"It's a trap! I   "

But it was already too late. Heavy boots thudded down the steps behind us. I couldn't see who they were, but I knew that there we too many too many enemies. We were trapped.

Thorne drew her blades and then ran the steps toward the chamber. I followed hard on her heels. Once on level ground, I stood at her right shoulder and stared at the occupants of the small, windowless room we found ourselves in.

There were three of them.

Two were dressed in the garb of Pendle witches, with tattered black gowns and pointy shoes. The third was a huge abhuman with too many teeth to fit into his mouth.

I faced three old enemies: Bony Lizzie, Mother Malkin, and Tusk.

· BOOK TWELVE ·

THE LAST APPRENTICE

I AM ALICE

Illustrations by
PATRICK ARRASMITH

JOSEPH DELANEY

GREENWILLOW BOOKS
An Imprint of HarperCollinsPublishers

The Last Apprentice: I Am Alice
Copyright © 2013 by Joseph Delaney
First published in 2013 in Great Britain by The Bodley Head, an imprint of Random House Children's Books, under the title *Alice*.

First published in 2013 in hardcover; first Greenwillow paperback edition 2014

The right of Joseph Delaney to be identified as the author of this work has been asserted by him in accordance with the Copyright, Designs and Patents Act, 1988.

Illustrations copyright © 2013 by Patrick Arrasmith

The text of this book is set in Cochin.
Book design by Chad W. Beckerman and Paul Zakris

Library of Congress Cataloging-in-Publication Data
Delaney, Joseph, (date.)
I am Alice / Joseph Delaney ; illustrated by Patrick Arrasmith.
pages cm. — (The last apprentice ; book 12)
"Greenwillow Books."
Summary: "Alice Dean's destiny is intertwined with Tom Ward's. But he's going to be the next Spook, and she's a witch—possibly the most powerful one the county has ever seen. To rid the world of its greatest evil, the Fiend, Alice will venture into the depths of the dark"—Provided by publisher.
ISBN 978-0-06-171513-6 (trade ed.) — ISBN 978-0-06-171515-0 (pbk.)
[1. Witches—Fiction. 2. Supernatural—Fiction. 3. Horror stories.]
I. Arrasmith, Patrick, illustrator. II. Title.
PZ7.D373183Iam 2013 [Fic]—dc23   2013024366

---

14 15 16 17 18 LP/RRDH 10 9 8 7 6 5 4 3 2 1
First Edition

 Greenwillow Books

FOR MARIE

I'm a bad girl, bad inside.

My hair is kindling; my flesh tallow; my bones dry twigs.

One day I'll burn in the fires of hell. As sure as eggs rot, that's the truth.

So there ain't no use denying it.

My name is Alice.

I AM ALICE

PROLOGUE

T HE destruction of the Fiend may be achieved by the following means. First, the three sacred objects must be at hand. They are the hero swords forged by Hephaestus. The greatest of these is the Destiny Blade; the second is the dagger called Bone Cutter, which will be given to you by ~~Stake~~. The third is the dagger named Dolorous, sometimes called the

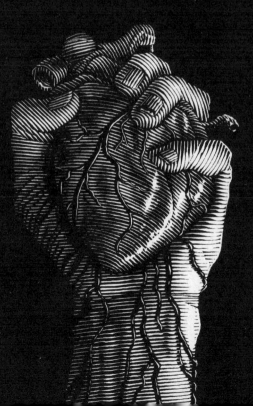

Blade of Sorrow, which you must retrieve from the dark.

The place is also important. It must be one especially conducive to the use of magic. Thus the ritual must be carried out on a high hill east of Caster, which is known as the Wardstone.

The blood sacrifice should be made in this precise manner. A fire must be constructed—one capable of generating great heat. To achieve this, it will be necessary to build a forge.

Throughout the ritual, the willing sacrificial victim must display great courage. If she once cries out to betray her pain, all will be lost and the rite will fail.

Using the dagger Bone Cutter, the thumb bones must be taken from the right hand and cast into the flames. Only if she does not cry out may the second cut be made to remove the bones of the left hand. These also are added to the fire.

Next, using the dagger Dolorous, the heart must be cut out of the victim and, still beating, cast into the flames.

CHAPTER I
A PRICE TO PAY

Into the Dark

Hell has many names.
Some call it the underworld,
Others Hades or the abyss.
We witches simply call it the dark.
It is our beginning and our end.

I was being trained as a witch, wasn't I, when I first met Tom Ward, the Spook's apprentice. We should have been enemies, but after a very uncertain start, we ended up friends. I helped him and fought the dark by his side, and it was during that time that I learned a terrible truth about myself—I was one of the Fiend's daughters, and

Bony Lizzie was actually my mother.

But I carried on helping Tom and Old Gregory, the Spook. Despite my background, I couldn't let myself go over to the dark. We fought the Fiend together, with the help of Grimalkin, the witch assassin, and eventually we dealt *him* a terrible blow: We chopped off his head and bound his body with silver spears so that he was trapped within his dead flesh.

Knowing that his servants would pursue us relentlessly, Grimalkin went on the run with the Fiend's head wrapped in a leather bag, fighting any creature she encountered. It would only be a matter of time before she was caught, I was sure—not even the powerful witch assassin could defeat so many dark entities. Once they killed Grimalkin and retrieved the head, they would take it back to Ireland and reunite it with the rest of the Fiend's body; then he would be set loose in the world once more, and a new age of darkness and terror would begin.

There is just one chance to stop him—just one way to destroy him forever. My friend Tom Ward has to complete a sacrificial ritual at midnight next Halloween, now less than four months away. It involves the use of three blades known as the hero swords. Tom already has two of these weapons in his possession, but the third is located in the dark, and it is up to me to retrieve it.

The details of the ritual had been communicated to him by his own mother, who was the first and most powerful of all the lamias. She died in Greece fighting the Ordeen, one of the Old Gods, but her spirit was still very strong, and she had been trying to aid us in our attempt to deal with the Fiend.

But there was something about the ritual that Tom had withheld from me. Something that I'd had to find out for myself.

It involved a sacrifice. There had to be a "willing sacrificial victim." Someone had to die.

Tom had to sacrifice the person he loved most of all.

That someone was me.

So I am off to the dark to find the dagger called Dolorous—the blade that will eventually be used to kill me.

Just one thing worse than the dark, ain't there? And that's what's inside it—the things that call it home. . . .

Lots of my enemies were in there, supporters of the Fiend. So I cloaked myself using the most powerful magic I had. I wasn't sure it would be enough. The dark is where magic comes from, and it's the dwelling place of the Old Gods. And I was alone.

I'd been there once before, snatched away by the Fiend. Each of the Old Gods has a home in the dark—a territory, a personal domain that belongs only to them—and there was one god who'd helped me. Brought me back to the world, he had. Pan. He, like some of the others, wants to be left alone, completely alone, and doesn't take kindly to intruders. If I found a way into Pan's domain, none of my enemies would be waiting for me there. 'Course that didn't guarantee that he wouldn't destroy me for invading his space.

Pan has two aspects, two different forms. One, which I hoped I would never see, is terrible. Most folk would be driven mad just by gazing into his face. The other form was the one I hoped I'd be able to talk to.

To get into Pan's domain with my powerful magic should be relatively easy. He mostly dwells in the dark, but he's also the god of nature. His home is never that far from our world.

Anyone who's been alone in a forest has sensed his presence. There are times when everything becomes still and silent; everything that *can* breathe seems to be holding its breath. There are no rustles in the undergrowth, no breeze; just a sense of a gigantic unseen presence.

Which means that Pan is close.

So I chose a forested area southeast of Chipenden, not too far from the River Ribble. If I *did* manage to get back safely with the dagger, I wouldn't have far to go to find Tom Ward again.

I selected a lonely spot, sat in the long grass, and made myself comfortable with my back against a tree. I was scared, my whole body trembling, so I took long, slow, deep breaths to calm myself. Then I waited for the conditions to become right.

It happened very close to dusk.

Everything became still and quiet, just as I knew it would. Pan was nearby. It was as if he were just behind a curtain, so close I could have touched him.

I used my magic and tried to enter his domain. It was much more difficult than I expected—it took me a long time to find a way in. It was like searching for a tiny lock in a big door with my eyes blindfolded. It was hard to locate, and it resisted my attempts for so long that I thought I was sure to fail. Then, very suddenly, I was in, and a mixture of feelings raced through me: elation at my success, nervousness at entering Pan's domain, and a touch of fear.

I was standing close to a lake that was gleaming bright green. Above, the sky was dark, so I knew it wasn't reflected light. *Everything* around me was glowing with that same green—even the tree trunks. Green is the color of nature. Green is the color of Pan.

At the river margin were tall reeds, and beyond them, on the far bank, thin ash saplings, but all was absolutely still. Nothing moved but my chest, which was rising and falling rapidly. I took three deep breaths, trying to slow down my heart.

I had to stay calm.

Just beyond the saplings was the edge of a forest—tall deciduous trees of a type I didn't recognize. They were covered in blossoms that suggested early spring, but rather than being pink or white, the flowers were green, too.

It was as if the forest were alive and listening to my fluttery breaths and the *thumpety-bump* of my heart. The word panic comes from Pan's name; they say that if he appears in his terrible form, a strong sense of dread is experienced at his approach. Few have lived to tell the tale.

Was he approaching in that aspect now? If so, I wasn't feeling the dread.

At that moment I heard high, thin musical notes in the distance. Could it be Pan in his more benign form, playing his reed pipes?

I could only hope for the best.

So I circled the green lake, pushed my way through the thicket of saplings, and entered the forest. I hurried toward the sound of the music and came to a wide clearing that was thick with ferns. At its center, they had been flattened by many creatures, hares, rabbits, rats, mice, voles, a couple of badgers, and a bushy-tailed red fox, while above, the branches were laden with birds. All were silent and still, held in thrall to the source of that exquisite music.

Looking like a young, pale-faced, fair-haired boy, Pan was sitting on a log playing a reed pipe, just as I remembered him. His clothes seemed to be made out of grass, leaves, and bark. The face appeared human, but the ears that poked out through his long, unkempt hair were elongated and pointy. I also noticed the green toenails of his bare feet. They were so long that each curled upward into a spiral.

The Old God looked at me and stopped playing. Immediately the spell of the music was broken, and the creatures of the forest fled, while the birds soared up into the sky, making the branches overhead dance. Moments later, we were alone.

He glared at me, and his face began to distort into something fierce and bestial. I felt a cold dread wash over me.

In seconds the boy would be gone and I would face his other terrible aspect.

"Please! Please!" I cried. "I'm Alice. Remember me? You helped me once before. Please listen to me. Didn't mean to cause any offense, did I?"

To my relief, the change stopped and slowly reversed until I was looking at the boy once more—though his face looked very serious, without even a hint of a smile. Then it flickered with anger.

"You assume too much," he snarled. "Tell me why I shouldn't strike you dead on the spot."

"Don't mean no harm," I told him. "Sorry to intrude without permission. Helped me once before, you did, and I'm really grateful for that. And now I need your help again. I have to fetch something from the dark, and this is the safest place I could think of to enter. Got lots of enemies here, I have. But I know they won't dare come here because of you."

"But *you* dared! And there is a price to pay for such presumption."

"I'll pay whatever you want," I told him, "as long as you don't take away my life. I ain't afraid to die, we all got to go sometime—but I need to give it to someone else. My life has to be sacrificed. Help me, please. I have to find a blade that's hidden under the Fiend's throne. Just guide me to the edge of his domain and let me escape back this way afterward . . . that's all I ask."

Pan looked intrigued. "And why is the recovery of this blade so important?"

I had learned that I was to be the sacrifice by scrying, but later, when Tom Ward lay unconscious, recovering from his battle with Siscoi, the vampire god, I'd taken the letter from his pocket and read it several times, so that I'd remember it. I saw no reason why I shouldn't now tell the god. After all, he already knew how we'd bound the Fiend. It was that weakening of the Fiend's power that had made it possible for Pan to return me to the world above.

"We need three sacred objects for the ritual that'll destroy the Fiend for all time—the hero swords forged by the old blacksmith god. They must be present when Tom Ward carries it out."

"These blades are known to me," said Pan. "And they have brought much misery and suffering to humans. Which one is hidden here in the dark?"

"Tom already has the Destiny Blade and Bone Cutter. The one I'm here to find is the one called Dolorous," I told him.

"Ah, but the Blade of Sorrow is by far the worst of the three. It would be better for humankind if it were not returned to your world."

"But by using it we can destroy our worst enemy."

Pan slowly shook his head and regarded me with an expression of extreme pity. "Foolish human—don't you see what will happen? You may be able to destroy the Fiend, but you cannot destroy the dark, for it will always find a way to achieve balance with the light. End the present situation, and a new equilibrium will develop. Destroy the dark's most powerful entity, and another will eventually grow in power and replace it."

These were not words I wanted to hear. Did it mean I was going to sacrifice my life for nothing? But that was for the long term; it was the situation *now* we had to deal with. What happened in the distant future seemed less important.

"If that happens, it happens, and I can't do nothing about it, can I? But we have already attacked the Fiend and hurt him badly. If he recovers and returns to his former power, his revenge will be terrible. Ain't just talking about me, Tom, and Old Gregory—the whole world will suffer. So we got to stop him somehow. And the ritual has to be carried out this coming Halloween, or it will be too late."

Pan stared at me for a long time, and my knees began to tremble. I had strong magic at my disposal, and for a moment I thought about using it, but I knew that I had no chance against one of the Old Gods in the heart of his territory. He might kill me on the spot, and all I'd done would have been for nothing.

Then he gave me a quick nod. "Tell me more about the ritual," he commanded.

"It has to be done on a special hill in the County called the Wardstone. A forge has to be built there," I explained. "The victim must not cry out, no matter how terrible the pain. The dagger called Bone Cutter is well named—that is the blade that will cut the thumb bones from her. If she cries out when the bones of her right hand are cut away, the sacrifice fails. After the bones have been thrown into the fire, a second cut does the same to the left hand. The other dagger, the one I've come to get, is then used to cut out the victim's heart, which is cast, still beating, into the flames."

"You say 'the sacrifice,' 'the thumb bones,' and 'the victim's heart' as if they belong to somebody else. But this terrible thing will be done to *you*! Do you not know this?" Pan asked me.

I nodded and, unable to meet his fierce gaze, lowered my eyes. "Of course I know. Detaching my mind from it is the only way I can deal with it. . . ."

"Do you think when it comes to the sacrifice that you *will* be able to endure the pain? When they cut the bones from your hand, your body may disobey you and cry out anyway. To be human is to be weak. For you creatures, some things are simply impossible to bear."

"Just do my best. That's all anybody can do, ain't it?"

Pan nodded, and for the first time he didn't look quite so angry. When he replied, his voice was gentler.

"You may be foolish, human, but you are also brave. I will escort you across my land and start you on the next stage of your journey."

We traveled in silence, Pan about five paces ahead, striding out through the trees. All was still and our journey seemed endless, for it was difficult to judge the passing of time in the dark. And that was a worry.

From my last visit I knew that time behaved differently here. It had seemed as if I'd spent long years as a prisoner of the Fiend, but on my return to earth I found it had been mere weeks. I knew the reverse could happen too. For all I knew, time might be passing more rapidly back in the County, where now only four months remained before Halloween. Even if I did succeed in retrieving the dagger, it might be too late.

The forest was beginning to thin out now, the large ancient trees giving way to saplings and scrub. Directly ahead I could see what appeared to be a vast, featureless plain, divided by a path that began just beyond the final tree. Beyond the green glow from the forest, the land was dark but for this narrow path, which was formed of tiny white stones.

"I must leave you now," Pan said. "Follow the white path across the abyss that lies between each domain. It will take you into the next one."

"Into the territory of the Fiend?" I asked.

Pan shook his head. "Who can say? The domains of the dark constantly shift and change in relation to one another. Nothing stays the same for long. But if you can eventually find your way back here, I will help you return to your own world. But you entered my domain without an invitation, so remember that before doing so, I will demand that you pay the price of your presumption."

I stared at the path for a moment longer, and when I turned back to ask Pan what the price was, he had already gone.

I was standing still, but the green trees were receding. As I watched, the forest quickly shrank until it was no larger than the moon back on earth. A moment later it was no bigger than a star, and then it vanished completely. Had it grown smaller or had it simply moved farther away? It was impossible to tell.

I was alone, and now all around me was darkness. I sniffed three times, checking for danger. All seemed well, so I stepped onto the path and began to walk, the stones crunching loudly with each cautious step of my pointy shoes. It was perfectly straight, becoming fainter and fainter until, in the distance, it appeared to be no more than a fine line. Only the white stones were visible. I began to walk faster, striding on.

Again it was hard to judge the passage of time, and I don't know how long I'd been walking when I heard a distant howl somewhere to my left. It sounded like the hunting cry of a wolf or some other large predator.

Suddenly nervous, I increased my pace a little, listening out. I became aware of the loud crunching of my shoes on the pebble path. If it was some sort of wolf and it hadn't sniffed my scent already, surely the sound of my footsteps would bring it in my direction? I decided to walk alongside the path rather than on it.

But when I tried to step off, my left shoe encountered no resistance. There was nothing there. No ground.

Pan had said that an abyss lay between each of the zones! And what was an abyss other than a great emptiness, a bottomless pit?

Pitching forward into the darkness, I twisted desperately and managed to fall sideways, back onto the path. Then, my heart hammering after that close call, I knelt and looked down. I could see nothing. On all sides was absolute darkness. With my left hand I reached down but could feel nothing. What could I do but continue on my way, keeping to the path?

My heart steadying to a normal rhythm, I crunched along, trying to work out the most likely explanation for what had happened. Either the ground had just disappeared, or the path had somehow climbed upward—in which case, what was supporting it?

The hunting cry came again. This time it was much nearer, but it came from below. So I *had* left the ground behind. I was safe from the creature for now—unless it could somehow find its way up onto the path.

Soon I heard the howl once more, higher and nearer, and I immediately became more nervous. Was it already up on the path?

I walked even faster, wondering what manner of creature was behind me. Was I being hunted? Was it some sort of demon?

I glanced back, and in the distance I could see something loping toward me on all fours. It looked like a small dog, but that might be because it was still a considerable distance behind me. I really had no idea how big it was. I began to run. It was difficult to get up much speed on the stones, and I slipped and almost fell headlong.

Risking another glance back, I immediately wished I hadn't. What was following me now looked very big, more wolf than dog, and it was gaining by the second. There was something strange about the creature's face. Yes, it had the bestial face of a wolf, but its expression was sly, crafty, and almost human.

A chill ran the length of my spine as, suddenly, I knew exactly what pursued me.

It was the kretch, the creature that had been created by witches to hunt down and slay Grimalkin as she carried the Fiend's head. Fathered by a demon called Tanaki, it had great powers of regeneration and had grown steadily stronger, learning from each encounter with the witch assassin. One of its weapons was a deadly poison that had weakened Grimalkin; only with the help of my magic had she finally been able to kill it.

Now it had a new existence in the dark.

And I was its target. I had hoped to sneak into the dark unseen but for Pan. What a fool I'd been! Things were watchful here, and this creature had found me already.

I didn't want to use my magic; it was a finite resource, and I might have need of it later. Not only that, each use of dark magic brought me nearer to being a fully fledged malevolent witch with a cruel heart of stone. This is what worried me most.

But here I had no choice. I decided to be economical with my power and use the minimum. I exerted my will, and a thick mist began to form across the path so that I could no longer see the kretch. I added to that a spell of bewilderment.

I didn't know how effective this would be against such a creature, but within seconds it howled again—no longer the triumphant cruel cry of a hunter; more of a baffled whine.

There was no knowing how long it would remain lost and befuddled, so I began to run again, until the mist and the kretch were far behind.

Soon I had something else to worry about, though. I realized that, in the distance, I could see the end of the path. The white line of stones simply stopped, and beyond it lay nothing but darkness.

What if I had become trapped in the space between zones? Did the path start and end with nothingness? I wondered. A dark rocky cliff lay directly ahead, and I saw that the white path didn't end after all; it simply disappeared into the mouth of a small cave.

Was this the entrance to the next domain?

A yellow light shone just inside. Unless I was mistaken, it was the flickering light of a candle. Who did it belong to? Cautiously I approached the entrance and halted, peering within.

A pair of vivid sapphire-blue eyes stared back at me. I saw a girl of about my own age. Her black hair was cut short, and she had a small tattoo on her left cheek—that of a bear. She was sitting cross-legged on the floor, holding up her hands toward me. She had been maimed—they were dripping with blood, and the cause was terrible. Where her thumbs should have been, there were two gaping wounds.

"You must be Alice," she said. "My name is Thorne."

CHAPTER II
THE KRETCH

T HORNE was the girl Grimalkin
had trained as a witch assassin. We
had never met. She had been kept a
secret from most people, but I knew
all about her, especially how she had
died. She had been slain by the servants of the Fiend on the edge of Witch
Dell. They had sliced off her thumbs
while she still lived, and the shock

and loss of blood had killed her.

The eyes that now regarded me with such seriousness were surprisingly gentle. But the lithe body crisscrossed with leather straps containing an assortment of blades marked her as a warrior.

"Do you know that you're being followed?" she asked.

"Yes. I think it's the kretch," I replied. "I used magic to keep it at bay, but it won't hold it for very long."

That was true. It was beyond death now. How could it be stopped?

As if the creature knew we were discussing it, there came another howl from the darkness, once again a hunting cry. It sounded very close.

"We must hurry!" Thorne rose to her feet. "Take the candle and follow me!"

I looked beyond her and saw that the cave opened up into a tunnel.

Thorne turned toward it, and I snatched up the candle and jogged after her.

Sometimes the tunnel was so low that we were forced

to bow our heads even when crawling on all fours. In one way, that made me feel better—for how could the kretch hope to squeeze through such a confined space? But then we would briefly emerge into caverns so vast that the candle could not illuminate the roof. There were ledges far above us, and I sensed malevolent, hostile eyes peering down at us.

"Whose domain is this?" I asked, shocked as my voice echoed to fill such vastness.

At my question, Thorne came to a sudden halt and turned to face me, putting her forefinger vertically to her lips to indicate the need for silence. Blood was still dripping from her mutilated hands.

"We are still in the place between domains, but sometimes the white path gives way to tunnels that are somewhat safer—too small to accommodate anything really big and dangerous."

"How big is the kretch, then? Grimalkin told me it was the size of a small horse. Can it follow us here?"

"It can and will," Thorne answered. "The laws of size,

matter, and distance are very different from those back on earth. It might well be catching us now. But there are worse things than its size. It was fathered by Tanaki, one of the hidden demons that dwell in the abyss. He too may come after us, but fortunately he truly *is* too large to enter this system of tunnels."

"Were you waiting for me?" I asked her.

Thorne nodded. "You have friends here as well as enemies. I will do what I can to help. But why have you come? The living should not enter the dark."

For a moment I hesitated. Could I trust Thorne? I asked myself. But then I remembered how positively Grimalkin had spoken about her. I had never heard the witch assassin speak of another with such warmth. Also, I had been alone in the dark and had not expected to be helped. My chances of success would be much greater with a brave ally such as Thorne alongside me.

"I need to find the domain of the Fiend," I told her. "There's a dagger under his throne. It can be used as part of a special ritual to finish him off. But what about you,

Thorne? How did you know when I would arrive and where to find me?"

"We'll talk later, and I'll tell you some of what I know of the dark," Thorne said. "There's a lot for you to learn, but now we need to reach the next domain. With luck it will be the Fiend's. Then you can get what you need and leave this place."

I would have liked an answer to my question. However, although I had spent time in the dark, it had been as a prisoner; Thorne had survived here. So, for now, it seemed best to accept that she knew more than I did and allow her to lead.

Soon we came to the end of the tunnel system, and the white path once more stretched out into the darkness above the abyss. It looked identical to what we had left behind. For all I knew, we had somehow come about in a circle and returned to the point where I'd first entered the cave.

Thorne led the way onto the path, so I blew out the candle and pushed it into the pocket of my skirt. "How long before we reach the next domain?" I asked.

She shrugged. "Everything shifts and moves here. It's impossible to say. I've not been in the dark very long. There are many who are much better at getting about, especially demons. They can get from point to point almost in the blink of an eye."

This was a dangerous and scary place. Thorne had found me; if she could do that, then a demon servant of the Fiend might do likewise. But it was no use dwelling on such possibilities. I had to simply deal with threats as they arose.

As we walked on into the darkness and emptiness, it seemed as if nothing existed except the two of us and the white path; that, and the rhythmic crunching of our feet on the stones.

It was difficult to judge the passing of time, so I began to count my steps to try and keep track. I'd almost reached a thousand when we heard the threatening howl of the kretch behind us. It had managed to get through that narrow tunnel!

In response, Thorne began to stride faster. When the

sound came again, she broke into a run, and I sprinted at her heels.

The howls became more frequent and louder. The creature was catching us. Thorne came to a sudden halt and turned to look back down the path. I followed her gaze. The creature was only just visible, but bounding toward us, getting closer and closer. All too soon I could see it in more detail.

It was as Grimalkin had described—similar to an enormous wolf—but as it drew near, I detected the significant differences. Although it ran on what seemed to be four legs, the front two limbs were like powerful, muscular arms, capable of snapping the bones of an opponent and tearing the flesh into bloody shreds. Its fur was black, but there were flecks of silver-gray on its powerful back. Set into its body were pouches from which the hilts of weapons protruded, but it also had sharp, poisonous claws. One scratch had almost killed Grimalkin, leaving her with recurrent bouts of weakness that made her vulnerable to her enemies.

I didn't want the same thing to happen to me now. I prepared to use my magic again, but Thorne had other ideas.

"Stay behind me, Alice!" she commanded. Then she stepped forward to face the kretch.

To my astonishment, she kicked off her pointy shoes and, balancing on one leg, reached up with her left foot for the leather straps that crisscrossed her body. Gripping the hilt with her toes, she drew a blade from its sheath.

The kretch was bounding directly toward her now, eyes full of anger and hate, teeth ready to rend her body. Thorne kicked out savagely, and the blade flew from her toes, skittering across the forehead of the beast, missing its eye by a whisker. She changed legs, now balancing on the left. This time the toes of her right foot selected a blade.

I admired her calmness. The kretch was almost upon her now, but the second blade sped from her foot and buried itself up to the hilt in the beast's left eye—right on target. It gave a roar of pain and reared up onto its hind legs, trying to tug the dagger out of its eye socket. It was then that Thorne dispatched a third blade and found the other eye.

Blood was running down the creature's face, matting the fur and dripping from its chin. Blinded, it slashed wildly at the girl, but she was no longer there. Howling with rage and pain, it lost its balance and fell off the path. The scream faded as it plunged into the abyss, getting fainter and fainter until it could no longer be heard.

I looked for Thorne to ask if we could be sure that the kretch was gone . . . but she was already running past me and sprinting onward. "Quickly! That could bring its father, the demon Tanaki, after us!"

We ran at full pelt down the path, Thorne carrying her shoes in her mutilated left hand. I was impressed by her despatch of the kretch, but from what she'd just said we were now in even greater danger. Tanaki might arrive in the blink of an eye; we had to reach the next set of tunnels.

Another cliff face was now in sight, the path disappearing into a cave once more. As we approached it, we heard a sound that became more worrying and scary with every step we took. It began as a low rumble but quickly grew in volume and intensity, until the small white stones on the path were shaking, juddering, and jumping.

"Those sounds . . . that's Tanaki!" cried Thorne. "He's big—really big—and the nearer he comes, the louder they will get!"

By now even the teeth in my head were vibrating. Then the vault of darkness above was suddenly sundered by blue-white lightning. The deafening crash of thunder was simultaneous.

"Run! Run!" Thorne shouted, sprinting ahead. "That lightning means he's almost here!"

Tanaki was still out of sight, but I sensed him getting closer and closer, and I ran at Thorne's heels, feeling that he might appear at any second.

But soon, to my relief, we gained the refuge of a cave mouth once more.

"We're safe for now," Thorne said, falling to her knees. "Tanaki never gives up, though. Each time we walk the path between domains, he will be hunting us."

CHAPTER III
WHAT MANNER OF CREATURE?

THORNE looked exhausted, and the blood still dripped where her thumbs had been. She tried to stand, but her legs buckled under her and she sat down again. "Sorry, but it looks like I need to rest up for a while. That took a lot out of me," she said.

"Ain't no problem. You rest until you feel better. That was a good trick, throwing knives with your feet!" I told her.

Thorne stared at me for a moment. "I've had to teach myself to do that. I can grip daggers with my fingers, but not half as well as I could when I had thumbs. It's painful, too—makes it hard to concentrate. But I was trained by Grimalkin, and she taught me to improvise and never to give up."

"Must have been good to be taught by the witch assassin," I said. "I drew the short straw—Bony Lizzie taught me, and I had to endure two years of cruelty and misery!"

"I could never abide her," Thorne said.

"Me neither!" I exclaimed with a smile.

"You didn't *have* to be trained by her, did you?" she asked me next.

My time with the bone witch wasn't usually something I liked to dwell on, never mind talk about. But Thorne's words had annoyed me.

"Easy for you to say!" I said angrily. "Ain't so easy to do, though. Didn't want her to train me, did I? But Lizzie wasn't one to take no for an answer. She'd decided to teach me the craft, and she got her way. That's how it was."

"Couldn't you have run away?" Thorne asked.

I had tried it on several occasions, but each time she found me and dragged me back. "Whenever I did, I suffered days and nights of pain, hunger, and terror as a punishment," I told her. "Used sprogs against me, she did. They tried to eat their way into my brain."

Sprogs were newborn entities from the dark, still trying to understand who they were and what their place was. They had tentacles with hooks, and sharp teeth, and could bite themselves right into your head if you weren't careful, forcing their way up your nose or into your ears.

"So mostly I did as I was told," I continued. "If Lizzie said study, I studied. She scared me with her magic, and I remember the cutting and the big sharp knife she used. Sometimes that hurt a lot. Got scars all over my body, I have. She took blood from me most weeks to help with her spells."

I glanced across at Thorne, who had put her hands over her ears and was shuddering, her eyes tightly closed.

"What's wrong?" I asked when she finally took her hands away and opened her eyes to look at me.

"When you said Lizzie came at you with a knife, it reminded me of how I died," she replied. "I have terrible flashbacks. The kretch seized me in its jaws and carried me to a mage called Bowker. Then witches held me down. I fought with all my strength, but there were too many of them. When Bowker sliced off my thumb bones, the pain was terrible, but there was something even worse. I knew it was the end of my time on earth; I'd never get to be a witch assassin like Grimalkin. And I wanted so much to follow in her footsteps. I wanted to be the best—the greatest Malkin assassin who'd ever lived. And all that was cut from me."

"I'm sorry," I said. "I didn't mean to bring back bad memories."

"It's not your fault. I just keep remembering how I died. It'll always come back to me, again and again."

There was a sudden noise from somewhere back down the tunnel, and we both came to our feet in an instant. Had

Tanaki sent something smaller after us? I wondered.

"We need to press on. The sooner we reach the next domain, the better!" Thorne said.

I'd expected to see the path again, but we emerged from the tunnel straight into what was clearly another domain.

There was enough light radiating from the purple sky above for us to see what a terrible place we'd arrived in. There were no trees and no grass, just a vast, arid wilderness scattered with rocks and boulders. The air was very warm, with a stink of sulfur, but not as hot as the ground beneath our feet. I bent and touched it, removing my fingers quickly. It was very uneven, with long cracks that vented steam.

This was a strange and terrifying place. I wondered who it belonged to. What manner of god would make this home?

Thorne and I glanced at each other and set off up the nearest slope. When we reached the top, I could see mountains directly ahead.

"We should head over there." Thorne pointed toward

them. "From higher ground, we'll be able to get our bearings."

"What is this place? Who would want to live here?" I asked.

"Well, that's a good question, Alice. You said you've seen Pan's domain. It's suited to him, isn't it? It must be green and lush because he's a god of nature. . . ."

I realized what she was getting at. "So what sort of creature would be happy living in this hot, barren wilderness?" I wondered. "Some sort of fire entity, no doubt."

Thorne nodded. "That sounds likely. Whatever it is, we don't want to meet it. It won't be long before the owner knows we're here and comes looking for us. We need to get out as quickly as possible. From the slopes of those mountains ahead, we might just be able to see our best route."

There was no arguing with that, so we set off just as fast as we could. Wasn't easy, though. Sometimes huge boulders blocked our path and we had to go around. We had a close escape when a jet of steam hissed up from the ground about ten paces to our left. Any nearer and it would have scalded our faces. It was so hot that we had to turn away.

At times the ground rumbled and shook, though not as violently as when Tanaki had come close. According to Thorne, he was mostly a threat between domains. Whatever was approaching was something peculiar to this place. I was thinking again about what sort of god would have this as his home when, as if she had read my thoughts, Thorne spoke up.

"Do you know what?" she said. "I think this is a new domain that hasn't been around for very long. Grimalkin traveled a lot and told me about her journeys. She said that she had recently visited an island full of volcanoes. The ground there was hot underfoot, with scalding steam just like this. The fisherman she forced to take her there told her that three years earlier there had been nothing there but sea; it was a new island born of fire that had burst up out of the waves. This seems to be something similar."

"That makes sense," I told her. "Maybe it's a new god,

only just born. Most gods are ancient, but they all had to begin somewhere, didn't they?"

Thorne nodded in agreement. "Grimalkin has her own ideas about that," she said. "She's learned things on her travels that those Pendle witches, set in their ways, wouldn't even dream of. She thinks that a demon can sometimes grow in power until it becomes a god, or that the reverse can happen."

I had always known that there was much I could learn from Grimalkin. Not only was she a great assassin, she had also acquired a great deal of knowledge.

"That's true enough," I agreed. "Old Gregory thought that about the demon called the Bane. It was trapped behind a silver gate in the labyrinth under Priestown Cathedral. Once it was a god, but because it was no longer worshiped, it gradually grew weaker."

"I suppose it depends on what people believe," continued Thorne. "If enough of them want something to happen, it will! You could well be right. Maybe a new god has been born here or is about to come into existence because of the worship of thousands of people somewhere back on earth."

I shuddered at the prospect of another dark god. Weren't there enough already? "Well, let's hope we never meet it," I said. "We must find our way to the Fiend's domain. I need to get that dagger."

We trudged onward, and I started to get thirsty—though I realized that I wasn't the slightest bit hungry. This might be the dark, but I was here with my human body. Surely it had the same needs as back on earth. I wondered what it was like for the dead. Did Thorne need to eat?

I tried to remember how I had managed when I'd been a prisoner of the Fiend all those months ago, but could bring little to mind. When I arrived, he had immediately handed me over to his servants. At first I had been kept in a cage, and I remembered a wet sponge being pushed through the bars into my hands. I had sucked on it eagerly, desperate for any drop of moisture. Sometimes the Fiend's servants had soaked the sponge in vinegar rather than water, and I recalled the intense, stinging pain as it made contact with my parched, cracked lips. Once they'd held me down and rubbed it into all my cuts. The memory made me more determined than ever to play my part in destroying the Fiend—no matter what it cost me.

Once again, it was difficult to judge the passing of time. Crossing the abyss, it had moved very slowly; here it flashed past, and it seemed to me that we were nearing the mountains much more quickly than we would have done back on earth. I could now see that their upper slopes were white.

"Snow and ice!" I pointed upward.

Thorne stared at the jagged peaks for a few moments, then nodded. "On earth, the higher you go, the cooler it gets. The same could apply in this domain."

"Snow and ice mean water!" I exclaimed. "Don't know about you, but I've never felt so thirsty. My mouth is so dry I can hardly swallow. If there's ice up there and it's hot down here, then at some point on those slopes it must turn to water. There'll be streams running down the mountainside!"

Thorne nodded again, not saying whether she was thirsty

too, and we hurried on. Soon we were climbing, once more picking our way between boulders and giving the crevices a wide berth. At any moment they could send up jets of scalding steam.

The closer we got to the mountains, the more formidable and inaccessible they appeared; soon they'd become too steep to climb. But then Thorne pointed to our left.

"There's a gap . . . a valley. Let's head for that."

It proved to be a narrow ravine, no more than a hundred paces across. Two sheer walls of rock confined us on either side. It was very gloomy, and the sky was just a narrow zigzag, far above our heads.

Soon we emerged onto a plateau, and I saw what I needed. So thirsty, I was! We had reached an almost circular area surrounded on all sides. At its center was a lake . . . but after one glance at the water, my elation turned to disappointment. There was no way I could even approach it, let alone drink it. The surface bubbled and churned, and steam rose up to form a cloud above our heads. The water was boiling.

"Ain't no chance of drinking that!" I complained,

suddenly aware that the ground was hot beneath my feet too. I could feel it through my pointy shoes.

"The water must come from somewhere to fill that lake, Alice," Thorne pointed out. "Most likely from the mountain peaks. There must be streams flowing down the slopes and across the ground toward it. They might be cooler."

So we began to follow the curve of the rock walls that bounded the plateau, moving to our right, widdershins. Soon we met a narrow stream, but it too was sizzling across the stones and hissing steam as it wound its way toward the hot lake.

"We should keep going," I told Thorne. "There might be something better farther along."

We jumped across the stream and continued in the same direction. Suddenly we got lucky. Water ran down the vertical rock and fell like heavy rain five or six paces beyond it.

"Ain't steaming," I said. "Don't look hot at all. Maybe it's falling from much higher up?"

I walked toward the waterfall and cautiously stretched

my fingers out into it. It was just mildly warm. Moments later, Thorne and I were both dancing around, getting soaked to the skin, laughing and shouting with happiness. I lifted my head, opened my mouth wide, and wet my cracked lips and dry tongue. Next I moved closer to the rock face, cupped my hands under the water, and drank until I'd had my fill.

It was then that I noticed something strange. Although Thorne was happy to let the water soak her and was busy washing her face and arms and hair, she wasn't drinking anything at all.

Didn't the dead need water and food?

But that thought was immediately driven from my head. I heard a sequence of clicks, like dry twigs being snapped underfoot. I looked about for the source of the sound. It seemed to be coming from the rock face, about four or five paces beyond the waterfall.

There was a narrow crack in the rock, and I could hear something inside it. Was it a rat? I wondered.

I was curious, but also very wary; I prepared to use my

magic if I had to. Then something gleamed in the darkness. There was a loud, angry hiss, and two menacing eyes stared into mine. I backed away from the crevice. The eyes had been large—far too big for a rat. What could be hiding in a narrow crack like that? What manner of creature was down there?

CHAPTER IV
THE SKELT DOMAIN

I watched, scared silly, as a twiglike thing poked out, making a curious circling movement as if testing the air. It was gray, multijointed, and very long indeed. It looked like the leg of a giant insect. As it lowered itself to make contact with the floor, a second limb followed, making the same spiral, jerky movement. When the head emerged, I knew immediately what the creature was. Its thin head and long snout were familiar to me. I knew them only too well.

"Thorne!" I shouted, for she was still under the water. "A skelt!" I didn't take my eyes off it as the rest of the spindly creature extricated itself from the crack.

The two segments of body were ridged and hard, as tough as armor. It was a cross between a lobster and a giant insect, with eight legs. As it stared at me, I felt the strength slowly starting to leave my body. There was power in those eyes—the ability to freeze its prey to the spot while it approached.

Skelts were very dangerous. I'd witnessed them in action, killing victims as part of a ritual practiced by water witches. They'd also attacked Tom Ward at the water mill north of Caster. Bill Arkwright had killed that one.

The long snout was a bone tube that it would stick into the throat or chest of its victims in order to suck out their blood. The creature was a vicious killer—bigger than I was, and a lot stronger, and very fast.

I knew I could fight it off with my magic, but that had to be a last resort. There were lots of reasons why I needed to keep my use of magic to a minimum; I had realized very quickly that I might need all my reserves to do what I had to do and escape from the dark.

The skelt was moving slowly toward me now, its joints clicking and creaking as it stepped delicately over the warm rocks. I could feel its power as it attempted to control my mind and freeze me to the spot as a stoat does a rabbit. I struggled and began to resist, but my strength was still draining away. Out of the corner of my eye I could see Thorne running toward me. She held a dagger in each hand, and her face was twisted with pain.

Before she reached the creature, it sensed her and turned, ready to meet her attack. I was suddenly free of its influence. This was my chance. I picked up a rock—a heavy one that I could only lift with two hands. Then I did what Bill Arkwright had done when he saved Tom Ward. As the skelt lifted its two front legs, ready to fend off Thorne's attack, I brought the rock down on the back of its head with all my strength. There was a crack, then a crunching, squelching sound as the skelt's head split open. Its legs collapsed under it, and it began to twitch and shake. It was dead or dying.

To my shock and astonishment, Thorne said nothing. She replaced her blades in their scabbards, knelt down beside the skelt, and began to lap the warm blood and fluid from its shattered skull.

I stepped back, horrified.

Thorne looked up and saw the expression on my face. Her lips were covered in blood. It began to trickle down from the corner of her mouth and drip off her chin. "What are you looking at me like that for?" she shouted. "It's what we need to keep up our strength. It's what the dead have to do in the dark. How else could we survive?"

She continued to drink the blood in greedy, desperate gulps, ignoring me.

Sickened, I couldn't watch. I turned my back on her and walked slowly away from the rock face, heading back toward the boiling lake. As I walked, I gradually began to calm down. Lots of Pendle witches used blood magic, but usually it was only small amounts. The rest of the time they ate normal food, like mutton, bacon, and bread. It was true that Lizzie had had a good appetite for rats' blood, but the only witches who gorged themselves on blood as Thorne was doing now were dead ones, bound to their bones, like those in the dell east of Pendle.

The rules must be different here—as I was starting to find out. This was the dark, and the dead here needed blood. How then could I judge or blame Thorne? She was just doing what was necessary in order to survive.

Although I was still some distance away from the lake, I realized that I could already feel warmth on my face. It was giving off far more heat than could be accounted for by the hot water flowing into it. Maybe there was volcanic activity directly below it? What if it suddenly exploded in a great surge of fire and boiling water?

I came to a halt. Suddenly I was afraid of the bubbling, churning lake. I sniffed quickly three times, trying to find out what threat it posed. I've always been good at sniffing things out. Some witches are better at it than others, but the skill came easily to me. It was one of the few things that seemed to impress Bony Lizzie when she first began my training. This time I was having difficulty gathering information. I tried again—three more quick sniffs.

I still couldn't find precisely what the threat from the boiling lake was. I felt that something might emerge from it at any time.

Then, as I watched, some small creature came crawling out of the lake toward me. How could that be? How could anything actually live in water of that temperature?

Another of the creatures emerged, and then another. Within seconds there were at least a dozen, all heading in my direction.

That was when I realized that they were not small after all. The lake was much farther away than I had thought. The creatures only appeared small because of the distance between us. But they were moving fast and getting larger and larger—which meant they were getting steadily closer.

Suddenly I knew what they were. The fact that they'd

been some distance away and had crawled out of a boiling lake had delayed that realization.

They were skelts, too!

I turned and ran back toward Thorne. "Skelts! More skelts!" I shouted at the top of my voice.

She looked up from where she was still feeding from the skelt's head, and at first did nothing but stare at me. I knew she was looking toward the lake, beyond me. She too would be able to see the creatures.

Slowly she came to her feet but stayed where she was. She was brave, Thorne, and I knew that she would wait until we were level before running herself. She was truly loyal—Grimalkin had made sure of that—and would not flee while I was still in danger.

I was right. As I came alongside her, Thorne gestured toward the plateau, and we sprinted toward it, stride for stride. We ran hard, and soon the breath was rasping in my throat—though Thorne seemed full of energy, her breaths still coming easily. Was that a result of the blood that she'd just drunk?

I glanced back a couple of times, but although the skelts still seemed to be following us, they were not gaining on us. I needed to catch my breath, so I paused at the edge of the narrow ravine, pulling Thorne to my side, and looked back.

The skelts seemed to have abandoned their chase. They had turned and were slowly moving back toward the steaming lake.

Why would they give up? Perhaps they didn't want to venture too far from their home?

Thorne and I turned and continued at a brisk walk.

"They came out of boiling water," I puzzled. "Skelts couldn't live in such conditions."

"Things are different here," Thorne reminded me. "These are skelts that died back on earth. Different rules apply. . . . Now that they've retreated, we need to climb again. We need to look for signs of the gate."

I didn't know what she meant. "Are we looking for another wall of rock and a cave to take us back onto the path between the domains? Is that what you mean by a gate?"

"No. Getting out of a domain is not the same as getting

in. An exit gate is so full of magic, it usually gives off a beam of maroon light. It's easy to see in the dark, but very difficult if a domain is well lit. Don't suppose it ever gets that light in this one, so we shouldn't have too much trouble. But we'll see it more easily if we're higher up."

Soon, after crunching up a windy, steaming path of volcanic rock, we did indeed catch sight of it. Thorne spotted it first but had to point it out twice before I saw it. It was a thin vertical beam of maroon light.

We took careful note of its position, then set off down the slope toward it. We were both nervous that the owner of the domain might find us before we could get away.

"Sniff it out!" Thorne commanded. "And tell me what it smells like."

I sniffed three times and instantly got the direction of the beam, which was invisible from our present position. There was a strong stench of rotten eggs.

"Eggs!" I cried, wrinkling my nose. "It's like stinky eggs!"

"That's right, Alice. So remember that smell—it's another

way to locate a gate. Sometimes you can't see the maroon light."

As we neared the gate, Thorne led me to the left, and we approached it at an angle. What had been a vertical line changed first into a crescent, gradually giving way to an oval shape. When we were standing directly before it, I saw its true form.

The gate was made up of three concentric rotating circles of maroon light floating in the air at about waist height. Through it I glimpsed another landscape—something very different from this volcanic wasteland.

Its position made it difficult to access. I approached it nervously.

"You have to dive through without touching the edge," Thorne instructed. "Catch it by accident, and you could lose a limb. The edge of the gate is sharper than one of Grimalkin's blades! You go first. I'll follow. Once you're through, go into a forward roll."

So I prepared to dive through the gate—into who knows what.

CHAPTER V
THE DOWNCAST DEAD

I threw myself into a forward roll, as Thorne had told me, and hit soft ground. She came to her feet behind me, clutching her blades, looking ready for anything.

It was night, but the air was warmer than the County on a summer's day. There was that same damp feeling as if, despite the clear skies, rain wasn't far away. It was quite a relief after the dry heat of the last domain. The sky was black and seemingly clear of cloud, though I could see no stars.

Directly ahead of us was a grassy slope. Without speaking, we began to climb it. As we came to the summit, I saw a full moon low on the horizon.

It was blood red.

I had witnessed such a moon before, on the night the Pendle witches brought the Fiend through a portal to our world—the same night the Malkin clan had sent their witch assassin to hunt down Tom Ward and kill him.

Somewhere ahead, I heard seabirds calling and, before we reached the summit, another harsh, rhythmic sound— the surge and ebb of the sea on a shingle beach.

At the top, we paused and looked down. Below us was what appeared to be a large coastal town. Its huddle of narrow streets sloped down to meet the wide curve of a bay. Fishing boats bobbed at anchor or lay stranded on the beach, where a red tide was lapping hungrily at the pebbles.

"Is this the Fiend's domain?" I asked, staring up at that scary red moon, sure that I was right and very relieved to have found it so quickly.

But to my dismay, Thorne shook her head, looking tense; I thought I saw fear in her eyes. "I've never been in the Fiend's domain, so I don't know what to expect," she explained, "but I do know where we are now. This is one of the most dangerous domains of all. It's where most of the human dead who belong to the dark congregate. It's full of dead witches and abhumans, not to mention demons and other entities that prey upon them. This is where I first came when I died. I got out of here just as quick as I could!"

"It was the blood moon that made me think this place belonged to the Fiend. It's like the scary one we all saw that night he came to earth," I said.

"That moon never sets here; it's fixed in one position. It's always dark. This is a terrible place," Thorne murmured.

"Ain't no point in going down there, then, is there? Best thing we can do is follow in your footsteps," I told her.

"We need to get out of here right away."

But Thorne shook her head. "I wish it were that simple, Alice . . . I *do* know the way out. There is only one in this domain, but it's in that ugly, dangerous town. If we want to leave here, we have to go into those streets."

This was bad. A town full of such entities offered a whole range of threats. And if the place scared Thorne—said by Grimalkin to be one of the bravest people she'd ever met— it certainly scared me.

"I could have lots of enemies down there," I told her. "Will they know I'm here? I did my best to cloak myself."

Thorne nodded. "Even with the most powerful cloaking imaginable, there are still ways, especially as you're still alive. It's very rare to see a living person here. It sends out strange ripples into the dark, and some of the dead will be skilled at sniffing out where you are."

"Wouldn't like to meet up with Bony Lizzie," I said. She was the first of many enemies who came to mind. There were lots of things that witch would like to pay me back for. I remembered how I'd helped Tom escape from the pit near Chipenden where Lizzie had imprisoned him. That had led to Old Gregory capturing her and throwing her into a pit in his garden. But she wasn't the only one I needed to fear.

"And there are others whose days I've ended or helped to end. They could all be waiting for me," I told Thorne.

Thorne wouldn't meet my gaze. She bit her bottom lip and turned her back on me.

"What's wrong?" I asked.

She swiveled round to face me. For a moment I thought I saw her eyes glisten with tears, but then I wondered if it was just a trick of the light. That strange moon had made it look like they were filled with blood.

"There'll be plenty waiting for me, too," said Thorne. "I helped Grimalkin for several years, and there are a fair number whose lives I ended with just my own blades. That's all the more reason to move quickly. Let's make for the gate without further delay."

What she said made sense. The longer we waited up here, the more likely it was that our enemies would be able to sniff us out. So we began to descend the slope toward the town.

As we walked, I decided to bring up the subject of the dead drinking blood. There were things that I needed to know, and I also wanted to make up for my reaction when Thorne had drunk the skelt's blood. It was best to get it out into the open and find out what the situation was.

"So the dead need blood. What happens if you resist and don't drink it?" I asked.

"It's impossible to resist." Thorne's voice was full of passion, and I knew she must have struggled to fight against it. "The hunger for blood just grows and grows until you can't resist it anymore."

"So what about me?" I asked. "Is the rule different for someone who enters the dark while still alive?" I had felt no urge to drink the blood of that dead skelt, only disgust. "The truth is, I ain't hungry for food at all. I just get thirsty from time to time."

"I've got bad news for you, Alice. All you *can* do is drink water. You can't afford to eat anything here. If you drink blood or eat anything at all, you can never go back to the world of the living. That's just the way things are here—one of the rules that you have to follow. It's not likely that you'll feel any urge to eat. But the truth is, at the moment you are using up your body's life force. That's what's feeding you. You're drawing on your own reserves. Stay in the dark too long, and you'd use it *all* up. You'd return a dry husk and wouldn't live for more than a few weeks—or even days. So that's all the more reason to find what you need quickly and get out of here."

It was usually good to know the truth, but every new piece of information made my situation appear worse. However, there were many more reasons other than my own survival to hasten my return to the County.

"You're right, Thorne," I told her. "I have to get back with the dagger in time to complete the ritual at Halloween. Grimalkin may be powerful, but she can't keep the Fiend's head out of the clutches of his supporters forever. There are too many of them, and they'll catch up with her one day. I need to get back before that happens. Is that one of the reasons why you're helping me, Thorne—to help Grimalkin?"

By way of reply, Thorne gave a barely perceptible nod. She had died at the hands of the Fiend's servants. No doubt revenge was another of her motives. Then I thought of another question. It was something I didn't really want to dwell on, but I had to know the worst.

"What happens to those who die here in the dark?"

"If the dead die again here, they crumble away to nothing and cease to exist. It means oblivion. After a while, some of the dead don't struggle to survive anymore. They'd rather be nothing than exist in eternal torment here in the dark. That would be my fate. But I don't know about the consequences for you, Alice. I've seen no other living people here. Maybe there are others who know what happens. . . ."

I hadn't intended to linger in the dark longer than necessary anyway, but none of this was good to hear.

It was then, as we drew closer, that I noticed something about the town below us. It was mainly formed of a network of narrow streets and small houses that led down to the shingle beach, but there were a few larger buildings. One of these looked a bit like a castle, and there was at least one church and a couple of what looked like warehouses that, back on earth, might have been used to store grain.

"Is that a castle?" I pointed at the largest structure, set on the very highest of the streets.

"No. That's the basilica—it's a big church, like a cathedral back on earth," Thorne replied.

I frowned in puzzlement. The only cathedral I'd ever seen before was the one in Priestown, the most important church in the County, which had a really tall steeple. This building had a square tower rather than a spire, but its size was impressive. What would a big church like that be doing in the dark?

"Do people in the dark go to church and pray?"

"Yes, they pray," replied Thorne. "But it's not like back on earth where folk say their prayers to God. As you know, the dead here mostly worship the Fiend, though some pray to other dark deities like the Morrigan or Golgoth, the

Lord of Winter. Well, there are altars to all of them in the basilica."

"There must be some who don't bow to any god—some who are enemies of the Fiend here, too?" I was wondering if somebody might be able to protect us as we traveled through this domain.

"There are a few who might just help us if we get into serious trouble," Thorne told me. "We do have friends here that we could call upon if our need is great enough. But I wouldn't count on it. We can only do that if our situation is dire. We'd be putting them in serious danger."

I could only hope that it wouldn't come to that. But I would do whatever it took to get the dagger back to Tom. "So whereabouts is the exit from this domain?" I asked Thorne next.

"The gate never stays in the same place for long; it drifts around. I know that some of the stronger entities here can manipulate its location. Sometimes they charge a price for using it. We'll have to search for it. We'll sniff it out eventually."

"But you left this domain once before, Thorne. Did you have to pay a price then?"

Thorne nodded. "Blood is the currency here. I paid them in blood."

I didn't like to think about what she'd been forced to do, but I had to question her. I thought I should know all the details of what I might have to face. But before I could speak, Thorne had turned her back on me and was striding along at a rapid pace.

We came to the foot of the slope, and the ground leveled out. Between us and the first buildings, which showed no lights in their windows, was an area of flat, soggy ground with a few dead trees and tufts of marsh grass. Thorne led the way, and we squelched forward, our pointy shoes sinking deeper into the marsh the farther we walked.

In the distance I could just see a few figures. The moon was behind the buildings, and it was hard to make them out in the gloom, but there were both men and women. They walked along, apparently aimlessly. One was going around in a circle; I heard a faint muttering but couldn't catch any words.

"They're known as the Lost," Thorne explained. "They don't know that they're dead, and their memories of earth are muddled. They're the easiest prey of all—their blood is easy to take so they don't last long."

At last the ground became firmer. As we left the marsh, however, I suddenly started to feel as if I was being watched, and the hairs on the back of my neck stood up on end. Twice I looked over my shoulder, but there was nobody there. Then, out of the corner of my eye, I saw movement.

"There's something over there to our left. . . ." I kept my voice low. A shadowy thing had seemed to rise up from the marsh but had disappeared as soon as I'd glanced at it.

"Just keep walking and don't look at it directly," Thorne advised. "Don't worry, the things that inhabit these dark dwellings and the outer marsh are usually the ones that aren't strong enough to survive in the town. It's most likely a glipp."

I had never heard the term, but Thorne explained. "It's a low-level elemental that likes mud and stagnant pools. A demon would gobble it up in an instant, and it's probably nervous about us, but I know that sometimes they get really hungry, and that can make them desperate."

We reached the first of the buildings—a two-story house with cracked windows and tattered lace curtains. It was dark inside, but I spotted a curtain twitching, and then something thin and gray moving away, back into the front room.

"That's probably nothing to worry about, either," said Thorne. "As I said, the most dangerous entities congregate either near the waterfront, or in and around the basilica."

I could only hope that she was right. She was the only friend I had down here.

We were now walking along a narrow alley between two stone buildings, but I could see lights ahead and hear the murmur of voices. Moments later, we emerged onto a busy cobbled street that sloped upward, away from us. Candles flickered behind windows, and there were torches on wall brackets on the dark side of the street, which was untouched by the baleful glare of the blood moon. But this was like no place on earth.

For one thing, rather than being gray, as they usually were in the County, these cobbles were black and shiny like cobs of coal. But the most sinister thing was the drain that ran beside the street, close to the houses on our left. A dark liquid trickled along it toward us. I gasped as I realized that it looked like old blood—the stuff that is swept from the floor of a butcher's shop when the day's business is over. I could smell it; there was a sickening coppery taint in the air.

There were people, too—the dead, who shuffled along with their eyes fixed on the cobbles. Mostly their clothes were in tatters, their shoes down at the heels. One woman with dark, matted hair had a red gash in her throat, from which protruded the hilt of a dagger; blood was trickling from it, and the front of her dress was saturated.

I glanced sideways at Thorne. Her mutilated hands were still bleeding too. So the manner of your death was carried over into the dark domain of the dead. . . . If I was right, then I might soon see far worse horrors than these.

"Fix your eyes on the ground!" Thorne hissed. "Otherwise you'll draw attention to us!"

I glanced sideways and saw that she was walking with her head bowed. I did the same, though I wondered why it mattered.

"Everyone is looking at the ground anyway, so how can they notice how we carry ourselves?" I whispered back.

"There'll be more time for questions later, Alice." Thorne muttered this so low, I could hardly hear her. "It's not these folk we have to worry about. These are what we call the downcast dead, poor weak souls who are mostly just prey. What do you think the strong feed on? These dead are just a source of blood—that's the currency here!"

CHAPTER VI
PREDATORS AND PREY

WE turned a corner, and another similar street stretched ahead, still continuing upward. There were more of the same shuffling dead, and more candlelit windows too—behind them, I sensed unseen hostile eyes watching us.

Suddenly I heard an eerie screech in the distance. I shivered, filled with dread. I knew I had heard that sound before . . . where?

The cry came again. This time it was much louder. Whatever had made it was traveling fast and heading our way.

The third time it echoed along that narrow cobbled street, I realized that it was coming from the sky. And instantly I knew what it was. It was the screech of a corpse fowl, sometimes called a nightjar; a bird that flies by night in the County. I'd used that eldritch cry myself as a secret night-time signal when I wanted to contact Agnes Sowerbutts. How could I have forgotten? Then a chill went down my spine as I remembered someone who'd had one as a familiar. Someone Grimalkin had killed and sent here to the dark: Morwena, the most powerful of the water witches, and another child of the Fiend.

The prospect of meeting her filled me with dread. She'd had great strength and speed, and a bloodeye that could freeze you to the spot while she ripped you to pieces and drank your blood. She'd been dangerous in life, and might be even more terrible now that she was dead. My heart began to race with anxiety.

The bird came into sight and swooped low over the roof-tops, its plumage lit to fire by the light of the blood moon. To my surprise, within seconds it had disappeared, and when I heard its cry again, it sounded some distance away. Was it still looking for us, just as it had searched for Tom Ward in the marsh near Bill Arkwright's water mill? If it had indeed spotted us, its terrifying mistress would soon appear. Of this I was certain.

With Tom Ward's help, Grimalkin had killed both Morwena and her familiar. And I'd certainly played my part in the days that led up to her death—as she would no doubt have learned from others in the dark. I was her enemy, and she'd be out for revenge.

There was one thing that worked in my favor, though . . . something that made the threat from her less immediate. Morwena's natural environment was water, and she could not survive outside a wet or marshy environment for too long. Away from water, she soon weakened. And this city was full of cobbled streets; the only liquid I'd seen so far was blood.

But what if the rules were different here? After all, she was one of the dead. Did she still need a watery environment to protect her?

Then, in the distance, from the direction of the basilica, I heard a bell begin to toll, each powerful chime vibrating through my teeth and jaw. It seemed that even the black cobbles beneath my feet were resonating with that terrible sound.

Thorne took my arm, pulling me off the street and into a narrow alley. She pressed down on my shoulder, indicating that we should crouch.

The toll of the bell stopped at thirteen. Almost immediately I heard a scream from farther down the street, and then, much closer, someone began to wail in anguish.

"What's happening?" I asked, keeping my voice low.

Thorne put her lips close to my ear and began to whisper. "That bell tolls frequently, but the precise time cannot be predicted, so it is never safe to walk these streets. The bell marks what is known as the choosing. If you are chosen to die again, you are summoned at the final chime—a terrible commanding voice booms out within your mind, and you must go directly to the basilica to be drained unto death."

"What if the chosen don't go?"

"Most cannot resist the voice, but in any case, it is better to obey the summons. Those who do so die their second death with little pain. Those who flee are hunted down without mercy and suffer a long, cruel end."

"Have you seen that happen?" I asked.

"Yes, once, not long after I died and found myself here. I watched a group of witches drag a man to the ground in the market square behind the basilica and slowly rip him to pieces. There were bits of his body strewn across the cobbles, but he was still screaming."

I cringed at the thought, but I sensed that there was something Thorne had not told me. I was right.

"This is a dangerous time for another reason," she admitted. "Immediately after the bell, there is a brief period when predators have a license to hunt whoever they like. A single chime follows, signaling that this time is over."

There were more screams from the street, and close by,

deeper into the darkness of the alley, I heard someone moaning—though whether in pain or fear, it was impossible to tell. One part of me wanted to investigate the sound and offer some help or consolation; the other was too scared to move. Even if I had forced myself into action, Thorne was still gripping my shoulder very tightly, and it would have been difficult to move.

Twice, something swooped low over our hiding place, first from left to right, and then the other way, as if it had missed us the first time but, sensing that we were there, had come back for a second look. It wasn't the corpse fowl, I was sure of that; it was far too big.

A moment later the creature returned, letting out a cry like the raucous screech of a giant crow. This time it didn't swoop over us. It hovered directly above our heads, and I had time to see it properly for the first time. It bore some resemblance to a bat, but it was at least as long as a human is tall, and extremely thin, with long, leathery, bone-tipped wings and glowing red eyes. It also had four spindly limbs, terminating not in feet, but in clawed hands.

"We are its chosen prey!" cried Thorne, rising to her feet, ready to defend us.

Whatever it was didn't look too powerful—though appearances could be deceptive. The claws were murderously sharp, and no doubt it had agility and speed.

Reluctantly I prepared to use my magic, but just when I thought the creature was about to dive and attack, a single deep peal of the bell rang out over the rooftops. In response, it gave a shriek, flapped its leathery wings, and flew away.

Thorne pointed to the entrance of the alley, and we rose to our feet again. "We'll be safe until the next time the bell chimes."

"At least the period when predators can hunt is short," I commented. Luck seemed to be on our side for now.

"That's true, but often a predator spots a likely prey and stalks it while remaining unseen. You never know where danger will strike."

"So that thing will keep track of us till the next hunting period. . . ." I realized.

Thorne nodded. "The entity that hovered directly above us is called a chyke. It's one of a class of lesser demons but is dangerous because it often hunts in flocks. It has marked us now and will be able to sniff us out. It might even pass on that information to others of its kind so that they can join in the hunt. The longer we stay here, the greater the threat."

"What about Tanaki?" I asked. "Can we be sure he won't follow us here?"

"There's a risk that he might come after us," Thorne admitted. "But mostly he haunts the path and the area between domains. That's where we'll be in most danger from him. That's where he'll be waiting for us."

We stepped back out into the street, and when Thorne bowed her head this time, I immediately did likewise and followed at her heels. Soon she turned left into an even narrower street, which climbed up in steps. Ahead, rising above the houses, I saw the threatening bulk of the basilica tower, bathed in the eerie light of the blood moon; we seemed to be heading directly toward it.

The dead were still shuffling along before and behind us.

Those heading upward walked on the left side of the street, keeping close to the drain and its trickling blood; those coming toward us kept to the right. All had downcast eyes.

"Where are all these people going?" I asked.

"Some are going to the basilica to worship. Others might be going to feed. There are blood shops, where victims are trapped and then slowly drained. A measure of blood is the reward for information regarding the whereabouts of someone who's fled the choosing. That happens a lot. It's dog-eat-dog here."

"What's the point of looking down and avoiding eye contact if predators can come from the sky?" I thought back to the chyke.

"Some of those who hunt are shape-shifters. They may be walking behind us in human guise, waiting for their moment to strike. Many of them have the power to freeze you to the spot with a glance, or plant a thought in your mind that will compel you to wait somewhere, ready for the tolling of the bell. So to look another of the dead in the eye is *very* risky."

"Could we be chosen?" I asked, filled with terror at the thought of hearing a voice in my head summoning me to the basilica.

"You're not dead, Alice, so you're safe enough—from that, at least. But, yes, *I* could be chosen. That's why I got out of this domain so quickly; that's why it's such a risk to come back."

I nodded, appreciating how brave she was being in volunteering to help me. In some ways, she was in more danger than I was. I began to wonder if it would be kinder to say thank you, send her on her way, and face the danger alone from now on.

Despite her warning about keeping my eyes down, I risked a glance upward at the basilica. There was something about it that made me feel uneasy. I had seen the citadel of the Ordeen in Greece emerge from a vortex of fire; I would never forget its three twisted spires, with their long narrow windows, through which I glimpsed demons and other entities moving to and fro.

I'd also been brought as a prisoner to trial in Priestown

and had stared up at the fearful gargoyle over the main entrance of its cathedral—the image of the terrible entity called the Bane. I had walked the labyrinth in the tunnels beneath it, and eventually had been held in thrall to that demon. . . .

Both were scary places, but this basilica of the dead, lit by the moon to the color of blood, terrified me in a different way. As yet, I knew not why.

The higher we climbed, the narrower the street became. The blood moon illuminated the rooftops, but the house fronts and cobbles were in darkness, the torches now few and far between.

There were also fewer of the dead around. Thorne had taken the lead, but I noticed that her pace was gradually slowing. Eventually she came to a halt and sniffed loudly three times. Then she turned round, and the look on her face terrified me.

"It couldn't be worse," she said. "The gate is now right inside the basilica."

"I suppose it ain't likely that it's just drifted there?" I

said. Did one of my enemies know I was looking for it? I wondered.

"You're right there, Alice. It certainly won't be here by chance," replied Thorne. "Powerful servants of the Fiend will have moved it there so that you will be forced to enter. They'll be waiting for you."

"It's a trap." I took a deep breath. "But I have to go on. Time is running out, and I have to get that dagger, whatever the cost. But there's no need for you to come too, Thorne. I'm grateful for your help—you've risked enough already."

Thorne raised her head and looked me straight in the eye. "There's another way, Alice." Her voice was soft. "I know a place where friends are waiting to help you—the ones I mentioned earlier."

"Friends?" I asked. "Who are they?"

"Some of them you might know; others are enemies of the Fiend, and that makes them your friends too. I wasn't going to accept their offer of help. I don't want to put them in danger. But now that the gate has been moved within the basilica, we have no choice. We need their help. They might know a way to get us inside without being detected."

"Do you mean there are secret entrances?" I asked. I remembered the tunnel that led from the ruined chapel into the dungeons of Malkin Tower.

"There could be. Some of these people have been here a very long time. They know almost everything about the dark."

I nodded. "Let's go and meet them," I agreed.

Thorne continued in the direction of the basilica until its massive bulk loomed over the rooftops. She led us toward a house that was larger than the others I'd seen. It wasn't terraced, but set back from the narrow cobbled lane on what appeared to be its own piece of land, full of tall weeds and nettles.

As we approached it, our feet squelched across soggy ground. The front door was slightly ajar, and Thorne didn't knock. She eased it open and led us through an empty room to some stone steps that led downward.

As our pointy shoes clip-clopped on the stone, signaling

our arrival, I became more and more uneasy. I could never have walked down *these* particular steps before, but they reminded me of something from my past, something scary and terrible.

We emerged into a cellar that spread out over a larger area than the old house above us. About half of it was taken up by a big pit full of murky water. I knew this place now. It was the exact replica of a certain cellar back on earth . . . a place I remembered all too well.

Against the wall stood a single large chair.

It was occupied.

Facing me was a large, podgy-faced woman with piggy eyes. Her hair was gray and unkempt. She was scowling at me from under her bristly eyebrows, hatred radiating from every pore of her body.

It was Betsy Gammon, an old enemy of mine. Someone who had plenty of cause to do me harm.

This was a trap.

Thorne had betrayed me.

CHAPTER VII
HOW IT BEGAN

To explain about Betsy Gammon, I have to go way back to my time with Lizzie.

I was born just east of Pendle in the shadow of that big, brooding hill. My kin were witches, and so there was badness in my blood. It was inevitable that I would be trained as a witch, and I had two years of learning the dark

craft from one of the most powerful witches of all—Bony Lizzie. It was a difficult two years. She taught me a lot of dark stuff, and there were things that happened during my time with her—things I've never told my friend Tom Ward; dark, scary things that led me to my first confrontation with Betsy.

One of the worst weeks I ever spent with Lizzie was when she took me with her to try and kill a spook.

I was down in the cellar of her dark, dingy cottage, studying. I heard the *clip-clip* of her pointy shoes coming down the cold stone steps. I was surprised. There was still another hour until midnight, and I wasn't expecting Lizzie until dawn—she had gone off to meet the rest of the Malkin coven.

I looked up from my book just as she moved into the candlelight. Wasn't a bad-looking woman, Lizzie, with dark hair and big eyes, but she scowled a lot. Muttered under her breath, too—spells and curses mostly—and I could tell she was in a foul mood now, because the corners of her mouth were twitching.

"That's enough reading for now. We're off to Bury," she said.

It was the middle of the night, and I wasn't best pleased by this news. I was tired and looking forward to crawling into bed. "Where's that?" I asked.

"It's a village not far south of Ramsbottom."

I'd never heard of Ramsbottom either. I'd lived in the Pendle district all my life and didn't know much of the County beyond that.

"Got work to do, we have. Dark work," Lizzie hissed. "Coven business. We drew straws, and of the thirteen, mine was the shortest. The witch assassin is busy elsewhere, so it's down to me now. I'm going to kill a spook. Deserves to die, he does. We cursed him before, but somehow he survived. Messed with us far too long, and now he's got it coming."

Lizzie must have seen the reluctance in my face, and she scowled at me. "Right, girl! You've dawdled long enough. On your feet, or you'll wish you'd never been born!" She stamped her foot. Immediately, nasty twitchy things with tentacles and sharp teeth began to form in the darkest corners of the room, places where the flickering light from the candle flame couldn't reach.

They were sprogs from the dark—those newborn entities, still trying to understand who they were and what their place was. Lizzie could summon them to do her bidding, and she was good at that. They could terrify, torment, or even kill if there were enough of them. I shuddered. Lizzie loved to use them against me—she knew how scared of them I was. The first time she set sprogs on me, she'd told me the story of a young Malkin girl who'd been killed by them. The witch training her had been old and a bit absentminded. She'd summoned the sprogs to punish the girl for burning the toast, but then forgot all about them. She was deaf, too, so she didn't hear the screams. And when she finally went looking for the girl, it was too late. Her brain had been eaten clean away. Her eyes were empty sockets, and there were bloody holes all over her where the sprogs had eaten their fill and left the body.

That was why I was so terrified. If I didn't get up right

away, the most powerful ones would come closer and start to nip and scratch. I'd have to close my mouth firmly and pinch my nostrils to stop any from getting up my nose. But while I was doing that, they'd be trying to get into my ears. . . . I just didn't have enough hands to fight them off. The pain would get worse and worse, while my panic slowly grew. It was a nasty experience, and I really believed that if I angered Lizzie enough, one day she'd walk away and leave me to be eaten.

So I closed the grimoire, Lizzie's oldest book of spells, got up, and pushed my stool underneath the table. As the sprogs started to fade away, I blew out the candle and followed her up the stairs.

We were off to kill a spook, and I didn't like the sound of that one little bit. This was well before I met John Gregory, Tom Ward's master. At that time I had only heard witches' tales about them—that they were our enemies and they fought ghosts, ghasts, boggarts, and malevolent witches like Lizzie. I believed that to fall into their hands was the worst fate possible. Some would throw you into pits and leave you to rot there for the rest of your miserable life. Or they might cut out your heart and eat it to stop you from coming back from the dead.

I did know that some spooks were better at their job than others. If this spook had messed with Lizzie's coven, which was the most dangerous one in Pendle, he was no doubt brave and knew what he was doing. Maybe sorting out witches was his specialty? In that case, he'd have a silver chain and lots of pits ready to bind his victims.

Didn't fancy spending the rest of my life in a pit, did I? But I had no choice, so I followed Lizzie out into the night.

Lizzie was in a rush. We set off south at a fair old pace, and I struggled to keep up. But just before dawn, we settled down in a wood to pass the daylight hours. I was tired and was pleased that Lizzie let me sleep right through until dusk, when she sent me out hunting for rabbits. I was good at that—been able to set traps since I was a little girl, I have. I also knew how to charm a rabbit. If you whispered in exactly the right way, they'd come right to your hand.

I caught two and came back to find that she'd already

made a fire, so I set to work cooking our supper. Sometimes Lizzie liked her meat raw—she had a taste for rats—but on this occasion she was content to eat her rabbit straight from the cooking spit.

"You're lucky to be coming with me, girl." She licked her fingers. "There's not many has the chance to see a spook get his comeuppance."

"How are you going to sort him, Lizzie?" I asked nervously. I kept imagining the spook catching me and burying me alive in a pit, where I'd have to survive by eating slugs, snails, and rats. Lizzie had taught me the spell to summon a rat, but I knew I'd never be able to face eating one raw.

"There's lots of ways, girl." For once Lizzie seemed pleased at my interest. "We could try cursing him, but that's slow, and spooks, being seventh sons of seventh sons, have some immunity to it. So we've got to get in close and do it the hard way. Best way would be to get someone else to kill him for us."

"Who'd do that?" I asked. "Would you put a spell on someone?" There were spells of compulsion that could make people do things against their will, especially men. Men are much easier to control than women. And Lizzie was cruel, with a strange sense of humor—especially when it came to men. There was a miller who worked just south of Sabden village, a big man with more hair on his arms than on his head. Whenever we passed, she had him running up and down on all fours, barking like a dog.

"Why waste a spell when you can get the spook's enemies to do it for you?" she snapped.

"Do we know any of his enemies who live nearby?" I asked. No doubt he would have lots in Pendle, but we were strangers here.

"That we do, girl, but not personally. Just their names. Annie Cradwick and Jessie Clegg—ever heard of them?"

I shook my head.

"Not really surprising. Both of 'em were daft enough to get married and change their names. But they're both from Pendle originally. And when their husbands died, they started to practice the craft again. This spook caught and killed 'em both within a month of each other, and now they're bound in graves in his garden. Once released, those two dead witches will happily do our work for us."

We set off south again and arrived on the outskirts of Bury a couple of hours before dawn. Dark as it was, it didn't take Lizzie long to find the spook's house. He lived about a mile east of the village, down a narrow farm track. I learned that the coven had been spying on him to search out his weaknesses, but I could see that the house certainly wasn't one of them. As Lizzie pointed out, its only defensive flaw was that it could be overlooked from a nearby hill. That's where we settled ourselves down to watch, hidden among the scrub and long grass at its summit.

The spook's house was two stories high, with an extensive garden enclosed by a stone wall that had only one big gate. Inside the garden there was a grove of trees; somewhere beneath their branches lay the graves of the two witches.

There were no lights showing from the house, but we watched until sunrise, then took it in turns to sleep, Lizzie doing most of the sleeping. Although we stared all day until our eyes ached, still there was no sign of life.

"He must be away," said Lizzie as the sun started to set. "We'll give it an hour, then go down and have a look around."

"Shall I catch us some rabbits first?" I asked. I was famished.

Lizzie shook her head. "Work first, eat later!" she snapped.

"What's the spook's name?"

"His name? What does that matter, girl? He'll be dead soon, and he won't need a name where he's going!"

"Not even for his grave?" I asked.

Lizzie smirked. "Won't be anything left of him to bury once those witches get their teeth and claws into him. Want revenge, they do, for spending years in the cold, damp ground."

The hour passed quickly, but I could tell that Lizzie was nervous. Witches like Lizzie use long-sniffing to detect approaching danger. It was something I'd found very easy to learn—to tell the truth, I thought I was already better at it than Lizzie. But it doesn't work on a spook, because they're seventh sons of seventh sons, so I knew she was worried that he might return while we were in his garden.

Darkness fell, but the sky was clear and there was a horned moon above, casting enough silvery light for us to see by. At last Lizzie led us down to the garden wall. The gate was made of iron, which causes witches lots of pain, so I knew she wouldn't want to climb over that. She gave me a wicked smile and nodded toward the stone wall.

"Over you go, girl. Be quick about it. Call me once you've checked that it's safe!"

Didn't want to take any chances, did she? *I* was the one who had to take the risks. Still, I had no choice, so I clambered up and, once on top, lowered myself carefully until I was facing the inside of the wall. Dropping the remaining few feet, I bent my knees to lessen the impact and rolled over onto the grass. Then I kept perfectly still and listened. I was nervous. It seemed a terrible risk to trespass on a spook's land like this.

I could hear a slight breeze whistling through the nearby

trees, but apart from that, and a single hoot from a distant owl, all was silent.

"Is it safe?" Lizzie hissed.

I sniffed quickly three times. It seemed safe enough to me.

I came slowly to my feet and called back that it was all clear. Moments later, after landing with a thud on the soft ground, the witch was standing beside me. "Nice to see you still in one piece," she said with a sneer. "Never can tell what traps and snares a spook might use to protect his property. Take Old Gregory of Chipenden—he's the strongest spook in the County, and he's got himself a powerful boggart guarding his land. It tears any intruder to pieces."

Without a backward glance, Lizzie set off toward the grove of trees. I followed in her wake, fuming with anger. I'd never heard of spooks keeping a tame boggart. Had this spook also kept one to guard his garden, I'd be dead by now. Lizzie had used me to ensure her own safety.

Once within the trees, Lizzie made straight for the spot where two dark boulders lay side by side.

"Annie and Jessie are buried underneath these big stones," she said. "Some spooks use iron bars to imprison a witch and stop her from scratching her way to the surface. But Jacob Stone's one of the old school, and a cheapskate at that. Boulders are free—you just need lots of strong shoulders to heave them into position over each grave, and laborers don't cost much."

So the spook's name was Jacob Stone. I started to feel almost sorry for him. No doubt the two imprisoned witches were like Lizzie, who I was pretty sure murdered children and drank their blood to gain power for her magic. I'd never seen her do it, but sometimes when she'd been away all night, she brought back fresh thumb bones from her victims and boiled the flesh off them in a bubbling pot. Some of the bones had seemed too small to come from an adult.

"Are we going to hire some laborers, then?" I asked. "Can't see how else we're going to move those big boulders and free the dead witches."

I was mocking Lizzie, because that was the last thing

she'd do. A witch like Lizzie never paid for anything. But she didn't detect it; I kept my voice all innocent. I guessed she'd use some sort of dark magic but had no idea what it might be.

Lizzie smirked. "What we need is rats, girl. Lots and lots of fat, juicy rats!"

With those words, she sat down cross-legged and began to mutter a spell. It didn't take more than thirty seconds before the first rat ran squealing toward her. It seemed daft to me. How could rats move big stones like those?

The rat, a big gray one with long whiskers, headed straight for her left hand. She gently tapped it on the head with her finger, and it immediately lay still. But it was still alive—I could see its belly heaving. Within minutes, Lizzie had thirteen rats laid out in a row. She dealt with each in turn in a way that filled me with disgust. . . .

Lizzie bit the head off each rat, then spat it out at her feet before throwing the body away.

After the first two, I had to walk away, struggling not to be sick. But I knew she'd order me back, and I wanted to go on my own terms so, a couple of minutes later, when my stomach had stopped heaving, I went back to find her on her knees before a small mound of rats' heads. She was chanting spells again, this time with her eyes closed. Everything had become really still in the garden: the breeze had died down, and all I could hear was the muttering of the witch. Then I heard something else—the drone of a fly, and it sounded like a big one.

I hate all kinds of creepy-crawlies, but flies and spiders most of all. I couldn't bear the feel of them on my skin, so I jumped back.

An enormous bluebottle landed on the glassy left eye of the topmost rat's head. The droning grew louder, and a frantic buzzing filled the air, louder than a swarm of bees. A dark cloud of flies descended on the severed rats' heads. They writhed and buzzed and feasted in a heaving mass.

Lizzie bowed forward until her forehead was almost touching the fly-covered mound. Then she uttered a word in the Old Tongue, and the flies surged up from their feast and swarmed as one onto Lizzie's head and shoulders, completely covering her face. But then a hole appeared, and I realized that she had opened her mouth wide. She stuck out her tongue, until that too was covered in flies.

I turned away and covered my ears with my hands to shut out that awful sound.

Next thing I knew, there was a tap on my shoulder, and I turned to see Lizzie laughing right in my face and licking her lips.

The flies had gone; no doubt most of 'em had flown away, but knowing Lizzie, she'd have swallowed a bellyful.

"You're too squeamish by far, girl!" she told me. "A witch needs to be hard. I likes eating rats anyway—loves the taste of their blood—and a few flies don't bother me much, although they're not as tasty. Why should flies worry me when I've got what I need in return? They gave me the strength I need to move those boulders!"

There was a weird glint in her eyes, something I'd not witnessed before.

"Something else you should know," she continued. "This power comes from a mighty demon called Beelzebub. One of the Fiend's best servants, he is—sits on his left-hand side. Best to have lots of different friends in the dark, and he's one of mine. Helps me out a lot, he does. Don't expect much back in return, either. But see what he's given me now!"

Her words made me shiver. Lizzie walked across to the nearest boulder and pushed, rolling it away as if it were no heavier than a sack of feathers. As the grave was uncovered, there was a wet, sucking, squelching sound and a stink of soft mud. Moments later she'd moved the other stone too.

I was astonished by Lizzie's display of strength. But it was one spell I certainly wouldn't be using—I couldn't bear the thought of biting off rats' heads and being covered with flies.

"Right." Lizzie pulled a knife from the pocket of her ragged skirt. "Now it's time to free those two dead witches. I need more blood for that, but rats won't do. I need human blood. So come here. You won't feel a thing!"

III

CHAPTER VIII
The First Scars

I froze to the spot. I didn't like the sound of that one bit.

"Come here, girl. I need your blood *now*!" Lizzie commanded.

Did she mean to kill me? I wondered. Was I some sort of sacrifice? Is that why she'd brought me along?

"My blood?" I eyed the sharp blade nervously.

"Can't use my own, can I?" Lizzie hissed. "I need to keep my strength up. Don't you worry, girl. I'll leave you just enough to keep your heart beating—although for a while it might flutter a bit."

With those words she seized me by the left arm and pushed up my sleeve. There was a sharp sting, and then my blood was dripping onto the grave. It wasn't over. There was the second grave to sort, and she made a cut to my right arm, too. Gritting my teeth against the pain, I watched the thick drops fall onto the damp soil. I was shaking, and my stomach was knotted with fear.

It was the first time Lizzie had ever taken my blood for her magic. There would be many more such occasions—I still have the scars on my body to prove it, though they're mostly under my clothes so they don't show.

As Lizzie pushed the knife back into her pocket, she shook her head. "Ain't that bad, girl," she told me. "Stop sniveling. Need that blood, we do, because we got problems here. There's a nasty trick that spooks use. Annie and Jessie have likely been buried head down so that, without realizing it, they've been digging themselves in even deeper. We might have to drag 'em out by their feet. But your blood will give 'em a bit of encouragement and point them in the right direction. They'll sniff it and make a special effort to get free."

Much sooner than I'd expected, I began to hear small disturbances from the soil, and then three fingers were thrust upward from the grave to our left, to writhe in the moonlight. Moments later, two whole hands were clear and the top of a head was just showing. Then fingers began to wriggle out of the second grave as well.

"Caused some trouble, has Jacob Stone, but he's been sloppy here! Must be losing his touch!" Lizzie remarked. "Buried them the right way up, he has. They'll both be out in a jiffy!"

It didn't take the two witches more than five minutes to drag themselves out of their graves. They certainly didn't need any help from us—for which I was glad. I'd seen a dead witch before, but these two started my hands and knees trembling again. Jessie and Annie probably hadn't been much to look at alive, but dead, they were just about the ugliest, most repulsive creatures I'd ever seen.

They were coated in stinking mud and their lank hair was matted and stuck to their faces. Jessie, the larger witch, had only two teeth, big ones that curved down over her bottom lip like fangs. Both had long jaws and narrow-set eyes that gleamed white in the moonlight. And both started to advance toward me, sniffing and snuffling, hands outstretched, long nails at the ready, with just one thing on their minds.

For them, I was the only item on the menu.

My blood froze inside my veins, and my whole body began to tremble. Dead witches are incredibly strong. Sometimes they just suck blood greedily until their victim is dead. Other times they go into a feeding frenzy and tear their prey to pieces. Terrified, I hid behind Lizzie. I don't know what I was hoping for—she merely laughed at my predicament.

"Had a taste of your blood, girl, and now they want some more," she gloated before turning to the witches. "Listen well, Annie and Jessie," she shouted. "This girl's blood ain't for you! She's done you a favor. Her blood it was that woke you up, and me it was who rolled back the two stones. Get you some rats, I will—enough to be going on with for a while. But it's revenge on Jacob Stone you need. You need to kill him that done you in, not this girl here. Drink his blood, and then you'll be free to hunt whoever you please."

With that, Lizzie muttered something under her breath, and many more rats began to run, squealing, toward us, not realizing that they were scampering to their deaths. It was a spell that Lizzie had already taught me, another one that I was very unlikely to use.

Lizzie caught each rodent quickly and thrust them into the hands of the dead witches, who soon began to bite into them and slurp their blood.

"Right, girl, while these two get their strength up, let's go and look inside the old spook's house. Never know what we might find there."

Lizzie led the way, and I followed at her heels, only too glad to get away from the dead witches.

The front door was made of solid oak, but the magical strength that Lizzie had summoned was far from spent. She gripped the handle and tore the door off its hinges, throwing it aside on the path with a loud crash. Next she pulled a stubby black candle out of the pocket of her long skirt and ignited it with a word muttered under her breath. With that to illuminate our way, we entered the spook's house.

I didn't want to be a witch and murder people and drink their blood—but, later, I had to admit there was something about Lizzie that one tiny part of my mind found interesting. In Pendle I spent a lot of my time feeling afraid and just hoping to survive. But Lizzie was so confident and competent as a witch . . . it would be good to be like that, in control of things and unafraid. It would be good to be strong enough to push away those who threatened me.

But those thoughts were far from me back then. I was nervous. This spook hadn't bothered to set traps in his garden, but what if there was something waiting for us inside? Lizzie didn't seem the slightest bit worried. She led us into a small room lined with bookshelves, all dusty and covered in cobwebs. It didn't look like old Jacob Stone had read any of his books in a long time.

"Let's see what we've got here," Lizzie said, lifting the candle high, her eyes starting to dart along the shelves of the spook's library.

There must have been a couple of hundred books, with titles such as *The Binding of Boggarts* and *Demons and Elementals*, almost all of them dealing with some aspect of the dark. But after a quick inspection, Lizzie seized just one and, blowing away the cobwebs, thrust it under my nose. It was bound in brown leather, and the title was on the spine.

The Practices of Malevolent Witches.

"We'll take that one with us." She gave it to me to carry. "It'll be useful to know exactly what a spook believes about us. I'll add it to my own library!"

I didn't really care what spooks thought about us. I just wanted to get out of this house and garden as soon as possible.

But Lizzie insisted on making a thorough search of the house, finding little to interest her. It was only when we reached the very last room, the attic, that her eyes lit up with what appeared to be excitement, and I heard her breathing quicken.

"Something special here!" she said. "Some sort of treasure!"

The attic was large, covering the whole top story of the house. Mostly it was being used for storage, it seemed. There were lots of open boxes, heaped with junk; nothing to do with spook's work, just discarded household items, and even a landscape painting with trees and a house in the distance. It looked like a scene somewhere in the County, because it was raining and a mist was rolling in.

However, it wasn't the stored items that Lizzie was interested in. She made no search of the boxes. After handing me the candle, she went down on her hands and knees, sniffing at the floorboards, her nose almost touching the rough wood. Serve her right if she got a splinter up her nose!

I sniffed three times very quickly myself, doing it quietly so that Lizzie wouldn't hear. She was right. There was something under the floorboards—something very strange.

"It's here!" she cried, coming to a halt at last. She thrust her hand down hard, and her nails tore into the wood. In one convulsive heave she ripped up a floorboard and tossed it aside. Another one followed in seconds. Then she peered down into the darkness and started searching the cavity with both hands. Moments later she lifted something into the candlelight.

At first I thought it was some sort of egg; a large egg, bigger than my fist. But then I saw that it was artificial, stitched into an oval from several pieces of stiff black leather.

"Bring the candle nearer, girl!" Lizzie commanded, and I did as she asked, stepping forward and holding it next to the leather egg so that she could examine it more closely. I noticed then that it was covered in writing that spiraled around from one end to the other.

"It's in a language I never came across before, but it's signed with a name at the bottom—Nicholas Browne. Wonder who he is? Might be written in a foreign language, but it sounds like a County name," Lizzie muttered. "Maybe it's some sort of warning."

She brought the strange object closer to her face and squinted at it, turning it first one way, then another, her mouth twitching. She sniffed it three times.

"I'm thinking there might be real power here; danger, too. That crafty old spook hid this away so that none like us could get their hands on it. We need to know where the fool got it and all that he knows about it. That means we need to keep him alive a little while."

Lizzie set off down the stairs right away. But she was too late. Just as we reached the door, we heard a terrible scream.

It came from the direction of the garden gate.

By the time we reached it, the two dead witches had already fed.

The old spook had hardly made it through the gate before

they'd leaped on him, dragging him down into the long grass and sinking their teeth into his flesh. Now Jacob Stone was drained and lay on his back, cold and dead, his unseeing eyes staring up at the moon. I felt sorry for him. He was old, far past the age when he should have retired from such a dangerous trade.

There was no sign of Annie and Jessie, but the iron gate was now open—they'd obviously gone off hunting, strengthened by the old spook's blood. They'd want some more. Some poor local family would be grieving soon.

"It ain't the end of the world," Lizzie said, kicking the spook's rowan-wood staff out of his dead hand. "If we can't question the living, then we'll question the dead!"

With that, she drew a knife with a sharp blade and knelt beside the body. I turned away in disgust, my stomach heaving. I'd never been present when Lizzie had done this before, but I knew that she would be cutting away the old man's thumb bones. Using them, she'd be able to summon his soul and get the answers she needed.

CHAPTER IX
THE RELUCTANT SOUL

WE set off toward Pendle immediately. Lizzie was eager to get back to her cottage and find out what the leather egg was and what it could do.

We arrived after dark, but despite her impatience, she couldn't get started on it right away. First she had to contact the coven in order to report back formally on the success of her expedition to kill the spook. I had a feeling that she wouldn't be telling them about the mysterious object she'd found hidden under the floorboards. That was something she'd be keeping to herself. And Lizzie was one of the most powerful witches in Pendle, well able to cloak her activities against the most competent of scryers.

So it was not until the following evening, just before twilight, that Lizzie finally set to work. She used the largest of her cauldrons, which was always positioned close to the rear door of her cottage. I was ordered to light a fire beneath it and then fill it three quarters full of water. That meant half an hour's hard work winding the bucket up from the well at the bottom of the garden. Once it started to boil, I stepped back and Lizzie began her ritual.

She positioned a wooden stool close to the cauldron and sat gazing into the steam that wafted up from the bubbling surface. Next she threw in Jacob Stone's thumbs; each made a splash before sinking toward the bottom. As I watched from a distance, she began to mutter under her breath, adding sprinklings of herbs and other plants to the pot.

During a ritual Lizzie would usually explain to me what she was doing and the purpose of each addition to the cauldron, but this was too important; she couldn't be bothered with teaching me now. As it happened, I already knew the names of most of the plants she used, and what they could do, and I knew that the crisis would occur when the meat softened and boiled off the bones. That was when she would try to seize control of the old spook's spirit and make him tell her the information she needed.

It was getting dark now, but Lizzie didn't bother lighting a candle. Soon I knew why. There was a faint glow from the inside of the cauldron; gradually it grew brighter, until I could see the witch's face clearly. Her mouth was twisted downward and her eyes were wide open, the pupils rolled right up into her head. Faster and faster she muttered the incantation. The water was boiling furiously now, and suddenly two white things bobbed to the surface, sticking up like twigs with the bark removed. Jacob's thumb bones were floating.

Moments later, the bones were lost to sight. It wasn't

because they'd sunk. The great cloud of steam from the cauldron swelled and grew into a huge thunderhead that soared to the height of the cottage. It was glowing, too, and I half expected to see forked lightning. Instead, a face began to form within the cloud—one that I'd last seen staring at the moon with dead, sightless eyes.

It was the spirit of Jacob Stone.

The first thing that struck me was that the old man didn't look in the least afraid. He stared down at Lizzie calmly and patiently without uttering a word.

It was the first time I'd ever seen her summon a dead person like this. When most people die, they have to find their way through limbo. After that, they either go to the dark or the light, depending on what they are and how they've lived their lives. Those going to the light find their way across in a few days at the most. That's why Lizzie had been so impatient to start the ritual. If a witch can summon a spirit, then she can hold him trapped in limbo indefinitely and cause him enough pain to make him do what she wants.

As a spook, Jacob Stone would know all about what a witch like Lizzie could do to him. He should have been terrified at being held in limbo at her mercy. But he wasn't, and that was odd.

"You're mine, old man! Mine to do with as I please," Lizzie crowed. "Just tell me what I need to know and I'll let you go. It's as easy as that." She got right to the point. "What's the purpose of the leather egg that I found under the floorboards of your house? What is it? What can it do?"

"I'll tell you nothing," Jacob Stone's spirit said. "All my life I've fought the dark and tried to help the good people of the County. Why should it be different when I'm dead? I'll do nothing to help you and your kind—nothing at all!"

"Won't you now! Then I'll make you suffer. Give you pain such as you've never had before!"

"I've suffered pain before and I've endured. I can do that again if need be!"

"Can you, old man? Don't you remember how in recent months your knees were starting to play up? So much so that you were beginning to develop a bit of a limp. It was the result of too many years walking the County lines in the cold and damp. The sockets were starting to rot away. Now it's getting worse. Can't you feel it?"

"I'm a spirit! I have no body. I have no knees!" Jacob Stone cried. "I can feel nothing! Nothing at all!"

Lizzie began to chant again, and the expression on his face began to change. The lines on his forehead deepened, and his face began to contort, showing that, despite his brave words, he was in extreme pain.

"Not sure now, are you?" Lizzie gloated, her voice ringing with triumph. "Your bones are grinding together inside their sockets. Your knees are starting to crumble. It's agony. You can't bear the agony a moment longer!"

Jacob Stone cried out and his face set in a grimace, but still he said nothing. Lizzie chanted again for a few moments, though I could tell that she was shaken by the old man's resistance. Suddenly, in a paroxysm of fury, she pointed at his spirit and stamped her left foot three times.

"I'm pushing a red-hot needle into your right eye!" she

cried. "Can you feel it twisting and piercing as it goes in deeper, inch by inch? Right into your brain it's going! Answer my question and I'll stop the pain. Then you can go on your way!"

The spook's spirit cried out in agony, and I could see a trickle of blood flowing from his eye, down his right cheek, to drip off his chin. But still he did not tell Lizzie what she wanted to know.

It was a terrible thing to see—for him to be a spirit but still feel pain. I felt sorry for the dead spook and wanted to walk away to avoid seeing even worse. But I daren't move. It would interrupt the ritual, and Lizzie would be so angry with me that an encounter with sprogs would be the very least of my worries.

Her face was filled with intense concentration, but I could tell, by the way her mouth was twitching and her hands clenched and unclenched, that she'd failed to break the spook. A witch can only use such spells in short bursts before becoming weary. Lizzie simply couldn't continue to give him such pain for more than ten or twenty seconds at a time. After that she would have to stop.

Releasing her breath angrily, Lizzie did just that. Then she began to pace back and forth in front of the cauldron with her eyes closed, as if deep in thought.

Jacob Stone's face was peaceful now. The pain had left him, and he was staring down at the witch, looking calm and dignified.

Suddenly Lizzie halted and a crafty expression settled upon her face. "You're tough, old man!" she said. "You can stand pain, all right, I'll give you that. But what happens if I hurt someone else? Have you any family?"

"I never married," he said. "A spook can't be distracted by a woman. He dedicates his life to his trade—to his vocation. The people of the County are his family!"

"But you are the seventh son of a seventh son, so you'll have brothers, and maybe sisters, too! And no doubt they'll have children. What if I bring one of your nephews or nieces here and hurt them? No doubt you'd tell me what I want to know to save that child pain!"

The spirit smiled. "You've failed again, witch," he told

her. "I was the seventh and youngest, but our house caught fire when I was still a child. My whole family died. My father got me to safety and then died of his burns. I have no family left for you to torment."

"Does it have to be family, old man?" Lizzie sneered. "Any child will do. To save a child from torment you'll tell me exactly what I need to know."

The spirit didn't answer, though I could tell by the worried expression on his face that she was right. Lizzie gave a wild, wicked laugh and muttered a word under her breath. Immediately the face vanished, and the cloud above the cauldron dispersed into the night air.

"He's trapped until I release him," Lizzie told me. "We need to grab ourselves a child tomorrow—maybe more than one—and use it to break his spirit. Now go and make me some supper, and be quick about it!"

I went inside and did as Lizzie had ordered, just pleased to get away from her. I didn't like the way things were developing. I'd known that Lizzie murdered children to get their bones, but to hear her say it out loud made me feel sick to my stomach. Once she'd used the little ones to get what she needed from the spook, they'd be as good as dead.

After supper Lizzie made me clear away the plates and then give the table a really good scrub. Once it was dry, she inspected it closely, her nose just inches from its surface.

"You've done a good job, girl," she said at last. "Can't be too careful. One speck of dirt could spoil everything."

That said, she went and brought the leather egg down from its hiding place in her room and positioned it right in the center of the table. Next she sat on a stool, leaned her elbows on the table, and stared at the strange object for a long time. She didn't move and I couldn't even hear her breathing, but a couple of times she gave a sniff. Doing her best to learn all about it, she was.

I had a bad feeling about that egg. It was dangerous, I was sure. Didn't even want to be in the same room.

"What's inside it—that's what we need to know," muttered Lizzie, more to herself than me. "But it don't feel right tonight." She gave a little shiver. "There are good times and bad times for delving into mysteries like this one, and sometimes things shouldn't be forced. Cutting it open might well ruin it. But there are other ways . . . I'll think for a while and see what I can come up with."

It seemed to me that it was always going to be a bad time to be meddling with that leather egg. But Lizzie would have her way. What could I do?

Putting an end to her muttering, Lizzie clutched the leather egg to her bosom and took it back up to its hiding place.

I wasn't sure whether to be relieved or disappointed. I was curious about what was inside the egg too, but a sense of danger radiated from it. It was best left alone—I knew that for sure.

CHAPTER X
BLOOD SPOTS

L<small>IZZIE</small> quickly became impatient once more. She wouldn't touch the egg, but as the sun went down, she decided to tackle the spirit of Jacob Stone again, forcing him to tell her what she needed to know about it.

As usual, the hard work of drawing the water, filling the big cauldron, and lighting the fire was left to me.

This time the bones were free of the spook's flesh. White and gleaming, they were, in the palm of Lizzie's grubby left hand. When she tipped them into the cauldron, they sank briefly but then bobbed up to the surface, just like the day before. Once again, the cauldron glowed and the cloud of steam rose above it—but this time there was one big difference.

The face of Jacob Stone was nowhere to be seen.

Lizzie muttered her spells with increasing desperation, but to no avail. "He's broken free!" she hissed. "Gone to the light, he has. Who would have thought the old man was that strong?"

I couldn't believe it either. Old Jacob Stone was really something. I wondered how he'd managed to do it. It made me realize that there was a lot Lizzie didn't know—she certainly wasn't all-powerful. Even a dead spook could give her trouble.

But her failure to make the spook's spirit tell her the secrets of the egg put Lizzie in a foul mood.

That night I didn't sleep well.

○ ○ ○

I got up early and went to carry out the first of my early morning chores. I began by collecting eggs, carefully searching the hedgerow on the eastern edge of the garden, where the youngest hens usually laid. I sniffed each egg twice to make sure, only placing Lizzie's favorites in my basket. She liked the ones that contained blood spots best—couldn't get enough of 'em. Once I had half a dozen, I went back to the house. Lizzie was usually a late riser, but to my surprise she was up already, waiting in the kitchen like a cat ready for the cream.

She snatched the basket from me, put it on the table, and selected one of the speckled eggs. After poking her fingernail into the end, she tipped back her head and poured the contents of the raw egg into her mouth. When she licked her lips, I could see big clots of blood on her tongue.

"A tasty egg, that!" Lizzie said. "It was nearly as good as a ready-to-hatch baby bird! Why don't you try one, girl?"

I shook my head, wrinkling my nose in disgust.

"You're a fool, you are, to turn down good food. Could

be all you get until tonight. No time for a cooked break-
fast. We're off right away."

"Off where?" I asked.

"You'll find out soon enough, but we'll be away for days
up north, where our slimy sisters live. . . . Let's hope they
don't take a dislike to you!"

I didn't bother to ask what she meant by "slimy sisters."
No doubt I'd learn.

I was never happy being trained by Lizzie; sometimes
it really got to me. I'd not ruled out the idea of trying to
escape, but I didn't feel confident of getting clear away.
She was sure to come after me and drag me back. Still, if
things were really bad and the chance presented itself, I
knew I'd take it.

Lizzie soon finished off the other eggs and then, after pushing me outside and locking the door, set off at a brisk pace,
heading southwest. I followed at her heels as the sun climbed
in the eastern sky. To the northwest lay the brooding mass of
Pendle. Long before noon we had skirted its southern slopes
and had reached the bank of the River Ribble.

Lizzie eyed the fording place doubtfully. "You'll have to carry me across, girl," she snapped, leaping up onto my back and wrapping her arms around my neck.

Witches couldn't cross running water. That was why you saw witch dams across most of the streams in the Pendle district. These devices temporarily halted the flow of water so that a witch could avoid a long detour. There was no possibility of doing the same to a river as wide as the Ribble; it would take all my strength and Lizzie's will-power to get her to the far bank.

I set off just as fast as I dared. I had to get her across before my energy failed. The stones sloping down from the bank were slippery, and when I reached the water it got worse. The river was quite high and was rushing past my ankles with some force. Lizzie started shrieking with pain, and her arms tightened around my neck so that I could hardly breathe.

I staggered and almost fell—the water was up to my knees now. Just when I felt unable to take another step, the ground beneath my feet sloped upward and the water level fell to my ankles again. We were almost there! We collapsed in a heap on the bank. I was trembling with exhaustion, and Lizzie was shaking with the pain and trauma of the crossing. She started cursing me fit to burst, but I knew that for once she didn't mean it. She'd been really scared. Few things terrify a witch like running water. Lizzie had been brave to risk being carried across that wide river.

We rested for an hour and then continued west. By early evening we were climbing a big hill that Lizzie told me was Parlick Pike. At one point she halted and gazed out across the valley with narrowed eyes, as if searching for something. In the distance I could see Pendle. Nearby was another hill of a similar shape, which she said was called the Long Ridge. Nothing moved in the valley but sheep and cattle. Then Lizzie pointed to a large wood to the west. Beside it was a cluster of houses; smoke from the chimneys drifted eastward with the breeze.

"That's Chipenden," she told me. "And on the edge of that wood lives a very dangerous spook. In his garden he has a relative of mine, Mother Malkin, still alive but trapped in a pit. She is one of the most powerful and dangerous witches Pendle has ever known. One day we'll come back here to rescue her and put an end to him, but it'll be much more difficult than it was dealing with Jacob Stone. It's that John Gregory I told you about—he's the most powerful spook who's ever walked the lanes of the County."

It sounded risky to me. I just hoped that Lizzie would forget all about it. Going up against a dangerous spook like that was madness.

We didn't tarry near Chipenden but pressed on north through the night, crossing more soggy fell tops before descending to skirt what Lizzie told me was the city of Caster. It was a place where they didn't take too kindly to witches, choosing to hang rather than burn them.

At least the body of a hanged witch could be collected by her family and taken to join the other dead witches in the dell east of Pendle, I thought. Burning sent you straight to the dark, with no hope of return. But either way, Lizzie wasn't keen to join her sisters in Witch Dell and was very nervous of the city with its big, ancient castle.

At last we reached a canal. I was tired, but Lizzie insisted on continuing through the darkness; she kept up an alarming pace along the slippery bank. Just before dawn she halted, her back to the water, and pointed across the fields.

"Over there, hidden behind those trees, is a water mill where another troublesome spook lives. His name is William Arkwright. He hunts our slimy sisters. One day I'll put an end to him, too—just see if I don't!"

I decided it was time to ask. "Slimy sisters? Who are they?"

"They're witches, girl, like ourselves in some ways but different in others. They live in water and slime. One could be down in that murky canal water, just biding her time. Any second now she could surge up, get her claws into you, and you'd be as good as dead. She'd pull you down into the water but drain every drop of blood from you before you could drown. Lots of water witches in these parts, there are."

I looked down at the canal nervously. Suddenly dogs started barking; it sounded as if they were in the trees that obscured the house of the spook called Arkwright, and for a moment I saw fear in Lizzie's eyes. But then her mouth twitched at the corners, her eyes filled with determination, and she set off northward again at a furious pace. Soon we left the canal, veering slightly west.

We spent the daylight hours sleeping under a hedge, and then, at dusk, we were off again. There was a moon, and in the distance I could see the sea. We were climbing now, and the higher we went, the more choppy water I could see, stretching as far as the horizon. I did wonder then if I'd ever voyage to other lands. I knew it wasn't very likely if I did become a witch. The sea was full of salt, and witches usually kept as far away from it as possible. And that's what I seemed destined to become.

A malevolent witch.

I didn't want that, though, did I? Such witches kill even little children just so they can gain power. That power drives them on, until all human feelings eventually leave them. They end up cold inside and capable of anything. No, I didn't want that.

Anyway, it was after midnight when we passed through a small village with a big church. Then we were climbing again, up onto the grassy fells. It was hard work, and soon Lizzie was cursing under her breath. I knew better than to ask where we were going—she was in a really foul temper.

But at last, when we were crossing a rocky bank and I could smell smoke, Lizzie came to a halt and dragged me close, her nails digging into my arm.

"Below here, in a stinky hovel, lives a holy fool, a hermit!" she hissed. "He's going to tell us what we need to know about that egg!"

"How will he know, Lizzie?" I asked.

She didn't reply, so I followed her in silence down some stone steps until we came to the mouth of a small cave. She walked in as if the place belonged to her. Before us was a figure with a tangled mop of hair that came down to his shoulders and a long gray beard, sitting in front of a fire. Lizzie stared down at him for a long time, but he didn't so much as glance up; just stared into the embers.

"Look at me! Look at me now!" she commanded.

The face slowly turned upward and he met Lizzie's gaze. Whoever he was, the man seemed calm and unafraid. I hoped she'd have more luck here than she'd had with Jacob Stone—otherwise she'd be in a bad mood for a month, and I knew I'd suffer.

"You're a dowser, old man. The best in the County, they say. I want you to do something for me."

"I'll find nobody for you, witch!" the man retorted. "Get back from whence ye came and leave me be. Your kind isn't welcome in these parts."

He was a brave man to speak to Lizzie in that manner. Didn't he know what she was capable of? Perhaps that was why she'd called him a holy fool.

"Listen to me, Judd Atkins, and listen well. Do what I ask and I'll leave you alone to rot in your stinky hole. Cross me, and I'll cut off your thumb bones and boil 'em up in my cauldron. Do you understand?"

Judd Atkins stared back at her calmly, without a trace

of fear in his expression. A moment later, all that changed.

Lizzie simply muttered a few words under her breath. It was a piece of dark magic that she'd already taught me. It didn't work against other witches but was very effective against someone like the hermit. It was the spell called dread.

I knew that in his eyes, within seconds, she would begin to change into something terrifying and monstrous, her hair becoming a tangle of writhing black snakes, eyes turning into two fiery coals brighter than the glowing embers of his fire.

Judd Atkins came to his feet in a rush, his face filled with frantic terror. He screamed like a stuck pig and began to back away from Lizzie. Then he fell to his knees, covering his eyes with the palms of his hands. His whole body was shaking, and he was moaning in terror of what Lizzie had seemingly transformed herself into. Dread didn't involve a real physical change; it was an illusion combined with a strong pulse of fear directed at the victim. But of course the old hermit didn't know that.

Lizzie slowly reverted to her normal appearance, and when she spoke again, her voice was softer and reassuring. It was almost as if she were speaking to a small child or a frightened animal.

"Listen, old man," she said. "No need for things to turn ugly. Just do what I ask and we'll be on our way. What do you say?"

Judd Atkins made no reply, but a low moan escaped his lips.

"Take your hands from your face and look at me!" Lizzie commanded, her voice developing an edge to it.

The hermit did as she ordered, with an open mouth and terror-filled eyes. "I'll do what I can, but please don't hurt me," he begged. "Who do you want me to find?"

"Nobody!"

"Is it something you've lost, then? Or are you looking for hidden gold? I'm good at finding treasure."

He fumbled in his breeches pocket and pulled out a short length of string, attached to which was a piece of clear, colorless crystal. "With the right map I can find almost anything. Have you brought a map with you?"

Lizzie shook her head, and by way of reply reached into the small bag she carried across her shoulder and pulled out the strange leather egg. "I want to know what this is. I want to know what it can do," she demanded.

"That will be hard. That's the most difficult type of dowsing." He stared at the egg, a dubious expression on his face. "All we can do is ask questions. And the answers will only be yes or no, in each case. It could take a long time. A very long time indeed."

"Sooner we get started, the better, then."

CHAPTER XI

DO YOU NEED BLOOD?

IN the corner of the hovel there was a small oblong piece of wood that the hermit used as a table. It had no legs but rested on four stones. Lizzie knelt before it, swept the plates and cups off with the back of her hand, then wiped the surface carefully with the hem of her skirt. Next, slowly and reverentially, she placed the leather egg on the wooden surface.

I couldn't bear to look at it. I'd a bad feeling that Lizzie was dabbling in something really dangerous. But it was a waste of time telling her that—before I knew it I'd have sprogs clawing their way up my nose and into my ears. So I kept quiet and backed away a little.

She beckoned the hermit across, and with some difficulty he knelt down opposite her, with the table between them. I heard his knees creak, and his face twisted in pain. He positioned his hand directly above the egg so that the crystal at the end of the piece of string was suspended just a couple of inches above it.

"I'm ready," he said. "Ask your first question. The crystal will spin clockwise for a yes and against the clock for a no."

"Does this egg belong to the dark?" Lizzie asked, wasting no time.

The crystal jerked into motion and began to spin clockwise. No surprise to me, that.

"That's a yes," said the hermit.

"Ain't blind, am I?" snapped Lizzie. "Shut your gob, old

man, and let me do the talking. Now for my second question. Can this egg bestow magical power on its owner?"

Once again the crystal spun clockwise, and for the first time in days Lizzie smiled.

"How can the owner get this power?" she asked, forgetting herself for the first time. Of course, it was a question that couldn't be answered by a simple yes or no, so the crystal didn't move.

Her mouth began to twitch at the corners, and her eyes rolled up into her head—which was a sign that she was concentrating, working out what to do next. It made her look uglier than ever, and twice as daft as any village idiot. I would have laughed if I hadn't been so frightened of that egg.

Suddenly Lizzie opened her eyes wide, muttered a spell under her breath, and spat into the old hermit's face. His jaw dropped in astonishment, but he gave no other reaction.

"I've wasted too much time on this foolish yes-and-no business." She stared into his face; by now his eyes appeared glassy, as if he were no longer seeing anything.

"Now you *are* the egg. . . . Be it! Become it now! Just tell me what I need to know!"

This was something new. I'd never seen Lizzie do anything like this before. Sometimes her power surprised me.

"What's this spell called?" I asked.

"Shut your gob, girl!" she snarled at me. "Can't you see that I'm trying to concentrate?"

Then she continued speaking, looking at the egg rather than at the hermit.

"I want your power. What do you need in exchange?" she demanded. "Do you need blood?"

The crystal began to spin in a clockwise direction for a yes.

"How much blood?"

The string didn't even twitch. Instead the hermit opened his mouth and spoke, but his voice was different now. It sounded like the growl of an animal, though the words were clear enough. They sent a chill down my spine.

"Give me the heart's blood of seven human children on the night of a full moon. Give me thirteen witches united in that deed, and I will give the one who holds the egg her heart's desire! More power than she has ever dreamed of. Once my need is met, let her think only upon what she wishes, and it will be done within seven days."

My heart sank, and my throat tightened against a feeling of nausea. Lizzie wouldn't hesitate to do what was required. Seven children were going to be snatched from their parents and slain so that she could get her way.

"That can be done easily enough," Lizzie said with a smirk. "Now tell me exactly what you are!"

"What I am is not for you to know," the voice growled from the throat of the hermit. "And remember that you cannot do this alone. It is the work of a full coven of thirteen combining its strength!"

I saw the anger in Lizzie's face. She didn't want to share power with her coven. But it seemed that she had no choice.

We left right away and set off down the hill. Lizzie seemed determined to cover as much ground as possible before dawn. Surprisingly, she left the hermit alive. I guessed she thought he might be of use again one day.

As dawn approached we were heading east, the sea visible on our right-hand side. We found a refuge in a small wood, and Lizzie sent me out to hunt for rabbits. When I came back, she had a small fire going, and I cleaned and gutted the rabbits and cooked them on a spit while she sat cross-legged before the flames, her eyes closed.

We ate in silence, but every so often Lizzie would shudder, her eyes rolling up into her head to leave only the whites staring blindly at the fire. When she finally spoke, she seemed to be just thinking aloud.

"Ain't going back to the Malkin coven with this," she muttered, lifting the leather egg out of her bag and clutching it to her bosom. "Not going to share *this* with anyone. The power's all going to be mine.

"But only two of us, there are, just me and a girl who's too young to count. So I needs twelve other witches to form a new coven. Witches who ain't too bright and won't expect anything but blood. They're dangerous to work with, our slimy sisters are, but it could be done . . . it might just work!"

Lizzie never bothered to explain her plan to me. She didn't sleep that day, and we set off well before dusk. We were quite close to the sea, but the tide was a long way out, and at first all I could see was mile upon mile of flat sands. Then I saw a group of people in the distance, heading toward the shore. There seemed to be a coach and horses down there as well.

"It's a dangerous shortcut across the sand," Lizzie told me. "Though there's a guide who leads parties across, including coaches. We witches have to go round the bay the long way, because at times you have to wade through salt water. Best move on, girl, before they reach the shore and see us!"

However, just as we set off again, there was the sound of barking from the party crossing the sands, and Lizzie pulled me down into a clump of bushes.

"Could it be? Could it be?" she whispered. "Might just be farm dogs . . . but could I be that lucky? Could I really? Sometimes things are just meant to be, and this could be one of 'em!"

I wondered what Lizzie was ranting on about. Great teacher, she was—always went to great pains to explain what was going on.

There was a tall man with a shaven head walking behind the coach, a big dog on either side of him. I crossed my fingers they didn't sniff us out, for they looked like huge wolfhounds.

"It's William Arkwright, the spook I told you about," Lizzie said excitedly. "He'll be off hunting our slimy sisters farther north. Could be away for days. He'll certainly need the tide to be right before he can cross the bay again. His place will be deserted—couldn't be better!"

Lizzie didn't bother to explain anything, but once the party had moved on, reaching the shore at least half a mile south, she led us forward again.

"Are we going to the mill where he lives?" I asked.

"We are that, girl. There's a marsh behind the mill that he keeps free of our slimy sisters. But it's a place that's sacred to them. While the cat's away, the mice will play, I'm sure of it. Every water witch for miles around will head for that marsh. And we'll be there to meet 'em!"

We journeyed on through the night until we came to the canal again and turned south along its western bank. Before dawn we left the towpath lest we encounter bargemen or anyone else who might identify Lizzie as a witch. But we didn't rest—if anything, Lizzie drove us on at an even more furious pace. By now the sky was overcast, and a light drizzle was wafting into our faces.

At last, about an hour before dusk, we reached the mill that was home to the spook. It was hidden by trees and surrounded by tall iron palings; a ditch marked the boundary of the garden.

I didn't like the look of that ditch. Lizzie was dragging me into danger again. I wished we could go home. "It's like the moat that encircles Malkin Tower!" I exclaimed.

"Aye, girl, that's exactly what it is, but it's a very special kind of moat. Arkwright dissolves tubs of salt in it to keep the water witches out." I wondered how we'd make it, but Lizzie didn't seem too bothered. "That won't stop us. Not as difficult a crossing as that big river. You could easily carry me across. Love to explore that old mill, I would. Old Jacob Stone had that leather egg. No doubt Arkwright's got something hidden, too. That's what spooks do. If they find something useful to the dark, they either destroy it or hide it away from us!"

Lizzie led the way around to the gate and stared at that broken-down old mill for a long time. I kept thinking she'd ask me to carry her across the moat, but finally she shook her head. I breathed a sigh of relief.

"I'm tempted, but I've decided it's not worth the risk, girl. Do you know what the biggest danger is?"

I thought for a moment, and then the answer came to me. "The dogs," I said. "If we cross the moat, they'll get our scent. Arkwright would be able to use those big dogs to hunt us down!"

For a minute Lizzie seemed almost proud of me. "That he would, girl. If those wolfhounds can follow the trail of our slimy sisters across a marsh, they'd have no trouble at all finding us. And we need to stay here until our business is done."

With that, Lizzie turned her back on the mill and led us along a narrow path through the marsh. Slimy bogs with clumps of reeds and marsh grass made up most of it; there were also dark, stagnant pools of water that looked really deep. It was slippery, and I was scared of falling in. And what if there were water witches hiding just below the surface of the bog? It was all very well, Lizzie saying that she was going to work with them and form a temporary coven. But they didn't know that yet, did they? They might just attack anything that moved through their territory. And because Arkwright was away, lots of 'em could be on their way right now. Some might already be here!

Fear heightened my senses, and I kept thinking I saw things out of the corner of my eye or heard the faintest of ripples or other minute disturbances of the water. Maybe it was just my imagination. Or perhaps it was some small nocturnal insects or water creatures. I could see nothing, but it would be so easy for a water witch to hide beneath that murk and slime, and I half expected a hand to come up out of the bog and grab my ankle. However, soon the footing became less slippery and squelchy; we were walking on dry land again. As we climbed a small hill, I saw a couple of stone walls and the foundations of a building at its summit.

"This is called Monks' Hill," Lizzie told me. "This was once a monastery—until the monks were taken and drained of their blood, one by one. This marsh used to be home to scores of water witches who did as they liked. Until the spooks grew stronger in the County, that is. Even now, but for Arkwright and his dogs, they'd soon be back for good. Ain't no doubt about that, girl."

Lizzie led the way to the top of the incline and hunkered down with her back to the wall, facing the marsh. I settled down at her side and followed her gaze. Nothing moved, but I felt very uneasy. There wasn't even a breath of wind, and a mist was starting to rise, its snakelike tendrils twisting up onto the lower slopes of the hill.

Suddenly Lizzie sniffed three times before giving me an evil grin. "They'll be here shortly, but I'd as soon watch 'em for a while without being seen."

Didn't bother sniffing myself, did I? I was sure Lizzie was right. I could sense danger approaching.

She began to mutter under her breath, and I recognized the cloaking spell.

"That should keep us hidden," Lizzie said.

I was confused. "I thought you wanted to form a coven with them?"

"It all depends which of our slimy sisters show up here," she replied. "Most water witches are stupid—little better than animals. In return for a bit of blood, they'll help me capture the seven children I need. But there's one sister who is really dangerous. I don't want any dealings with her. She'd want the egg all for herself. Her name is Morwena, and her father was the Fiend himself. No, we don't want her to see us!"

As Lizzie spoke the name Morwena, a ripple of cold fear ran right up my spine. I felt sure I'd heard that name before; it was as if someone had walked over my grave.

I was surprised to see fear in Lizzie's eyes too. "How dangerous is she?" I asked. "Has she powerful dark magic?"

"Aye, that she has, girl. She's stronger and faster than any of her sisters, and she has a deadly weapon—a blood-filled eye. One glance and you're paralyzed, rooted to the spot like a defenseless tree before a forester with a big, sharp ax. You're helpless while she sinks her sharp fangs into your throat. So if we see her here tonight, we'll leave and look elsewhere for the help I need."

We waited in silence until darkness fell and we could no longer see the edge of the marsh. But the sky was clearing, and soon a moon shone down, bathing the whole area in its silvery light.

All at once I saw a movement below—and this time I wasn't imagining it. A ripple on the water, the lightest of splashes, and then a dark shape dragged itself up onto dry ground at the foot of the hill. It was the first of the water witches, and she stood with her back to us, water dripping from her tattered clothes, which seemed to be composed of weed and slime rather than cloth.

Suddenly she turned in our direction and sniffed very

loudly, as if searching for us. I held my breath, but Lizzie's cloaking magic proved strong enough. The witch turned back to face the water, but not before I'd glimpsed the long fangs protruding from her open mouth and the sharp talons that sprouted from each finger. And then I noticed that each of her forefingers was exceptionally long.

Soon other water witches joined her on the bank, and they began to talk. I say talk, but it was hardly speech. I recognized a few words, such as "hungry" and "blood," but mostly it was just a series of grunts and belches.

I had always looked down on most of the Malkins. The stench of their cottages, with the heaps of bones left in the sink or by the door, turned my stomach, but these creatures were far worse. Lizzie was right. These water witches were little better than animals. Did we really want to be teaming up with them? I asked myself.

Soon there were about a dozen witches dripping on the edge of the marsh; a few were dragging something strange onto the bank. It was a tubular wooden cage, about one and a half times the length of a tall man but considerably narrower than a human torso. Within it, something was moving.

And more was to come. The next three witches to emerge from the water brought prisoners with them: two men and a woman, who looked half drowned. They were choking and sputtering, the whites of their eyes showing, and covered in bog slime from head to toe. They were thrown down into the mud without ceremony, rolled onto their backs, dragged about ten paces away from one another, and arranged in a row. Next, short stakes were driven into the ground a little way from their heads and feet. Then, quickly and efficiently, their arms and legs were bound to the stakes with narrow twine. The two men were hardly breathing now, but the woman groaned as the twine was pulled taut, stretching her arms and legs wide.

The witches formed a line on the bank facing the prisoners. This meant that they were now looking toward Lizzie and me too. As they joined hands and began to chant, I wondered whether their combined magical power might allow them to see through the magical cloak the Lizzie had summoned. That made me nervous.

Wasn't bad at cloaking spells myself, but as much as I wanted to, I daren't add mine to hers. Take it as an insult, she would—it would seem like I doubted her.

I needn't have worried. Her magic proved strong enough. Soon the water witches stopped chanting, and one of them left the line. This one did not approach the prisoners, as I had assumed she would. She made directly for the wooden cage. In seconds she had opened a hinged door at the end; then she rejoined her slimy companions.

I stared at the cage, fascinated. For a few moments nothing moved. Then something slowly emerged from the open door. It looked like a large insect and stepped delicately on spindly legs. All at once I saw its elongated head, and I began to tremble with fear. It had a long, thin snout, which I knew was called a bone tube. I had never seen such a creature in the flesh before, but I had seen drawings in a book from Lizzie's small library about dark magic.

This creature was a skelt.

For a moment it seemed to be looking right at me.

Suddenly it gave a loud hiss and turned to face the three captives. With a shrug, it appeared to grow larger and, on eight multijointed legs, scuttled toward the nearer man. It thrust its long snout into his chest, and the victim cried out in pain. Immediately I saw the bone tube darken. If I had been watching by sunlight rather than moonlight, I knew I would have seen the transparent tube turn a bright red. The creature was sucking up blood from its victim at an alarming rate.

After that first cry of pain, the victim merely gave a series of moans, which gradually became weaker. When the skelt withdrew its bone tube, the man gave a loud gasp and a sigh. I knew he had taken his final breath.

Now the skelt turned its attention to the next in line. This was the woman; she began to struggle against her bonds and scream at the top of her voice. But in vain: The skelt was upon her in seconds, this time thrusting its sharp snout into her neck. Once more the tube darkened, and the woman's screams became a choking gurgle—until the skelt had drained her of blood, and she twitched and lay still.

The third victim did not scream or struggle. He began to pray out loud.

"Father, forgive them!" he cried into the night. "Let them see the error of their ways and turn away from the darkness. I accept the pain of my death. Use it to lessen the pain of others."

I wondered if he was a priest. But priest, farmer, innkeeper, or bargeman, it made no difference to the predator which scrambled up onto his body. The man tried to speak again, but instead his body convulsed as the skelt stabbed his neck. Soon he too lay still.

The skelt moved slowly away from his body, and then turned toward the still and silent line of witches, who were staring at it as if waiting for something.

Surely it wasn't going to attack *them*? I thought. How much blood did the terrible creature need?

But it was not the skelt that attacked.

It was the witches!

They surged toward us, madness in their eyes.

CHAPTER XII
BETSY GAMMON

FOR a heart-stopping moment I thought Lizzie and I were their targets. But I was wrong. As if at some silent, invisible signal, they ran toward the skelt, mouths wide, showing their sharp fangs. They stretched their hands out toward it; long talons gleamed in the moonlight.

The creature tried to scuttle through

the surging throng to reach the water, but there were too many of them and they were too fast.

Ferociously they fell upon the skelt and, to my horror, began to tear it to pieces. Arms, legs, and head were ripped from the body as blood began to pool on the muddy ground—no doubt its own blood as well as that of the three people it had gorged itself on. Like some insects, its body was divided into two segments, and these were quickly sundered by the taloned hands. Even afterward, the legs and body segments continued to twitch.

I realized that these water witches were exceptionally strong and wondered how Lizzie dared to try and enlist them in her cause. What if they turned on us? All her magic would be useless against so many fierce creatures who seemed hardly human at all.

For now they were feeding upon the remains of the skelt, breaking into its body cavities to feed, splitting its limbs with their teeth to strip the meat from within.

I watched them, revolted and yet unable to pull my gaze away from the sight. It was then that I heard the barking. . . .

The witches looked up from their frantic feeding. Now, in addition to the baying of approaching dogs, I could hear the pounding of heavy boots.

"It's Arkwright and those wolfhounds, back sooner than we expected!" Lizzie hissed into my ear. "Whatever you do, girl, don't move and don't make a sound. The cloak should protect us from the spook, but the biggest danger is that the dogs might sniff us out. With luck they'll be too busy biting pieces out of our slimy sisters!"

As the dogs emerged from the mist, teeth gleaming in the moonlight, saliva dripping from their open jaws, most of the witches ran for the water. They entered quickly, with hardly a splash, submerged, and disappeared from sight.

For some reason, about five of them sprinted along another path into the marsh. I thought they were going to escape too, but the last one left it too late.

The first wolfhound seized her ankle in its jaws. She fell to her knees but struck back viciously at the animal. The long talons would have sliced open its head, but just in time, the second dog leaped onto her and gripped her wrist firmly in its jaws, shaking it like a rat.

The dogs looked capable of finishing her off, and she began to shriek and thrash, trying to drag herself back toward the water's edge. But then the shaven-headed spook emerged from the mist and, with a curse, clubbed the witch with his long staff, striking her on the back of the skull. She went limp, and without hesitation he seized her by her long, matted hair.

"Good girl! Good lad!" he exclaimed. "Now let go and we'll take her back and put her where she rightly belongs!"

At that, the dogs obediently relinquished their prey, and Arkwright began to drag the witch away by the legs, her head bouncing along the muddy path.

Lizzie grinned at the sight of this. I couldn't understand it. This spook was the enemy of witches. It could just as easily be our heads banging on the ground.

Within moments, spook, water witch, and hounds had vanished into the mist.

When the sounds of their retreat had faded away, Lizzie

turned toward me and twisted her face into an evil smile. "Well, girl, this could work out better than I expected!" she said, full of glee.

"I don't understand. Doesn't this spoil your plan?" I asked.

"Be patient and I'll explain later. Just keep still and be quiet."

But I was curious and couldn't resist asking Lizzie a question.

"Why did the witches let the skelt feed first, before taking the victims' blood at secondhand?" I asked. "They're really strong. They could have ripped those people to pieces with their bare hands!"

"Of course they could, girl!" Lizzie snapped. "But that's part of their ritual, ain't it? Taking human blood that the skelt has already sucked up triples the strength of the magic."

After about half an hour, to my dismay, I once more heard the barking of the dogs getting louder and louder.

"They must have our scent," I told Lizzie nervously. "Let's run for it!"

"You stay put, girl. Got scents aplenty, they have, but they ain't ours, don't you worry."

I didn't understand how she could be so sure. Once more the dogs bounded out of the mist, the grim-faced spook hard on their heels. For one heart-stopping moment I thought they were going to run right at us, but then the dogs halted on the bank near the cage, sniffing at the blood-soaked ground and moving in widening circles.

Within moments they had bounded away down the path taken by the escaping witches, and Arkwright followed, gripping his staff, his face hard with determination.

When at last the sound of their pursuit faded away into the distance, I whispered to Lizzie, "Wouldn't like to meet *him* on a dark night."

"You ain't spoken a truer word, girl. They don't come any meaner. It's one thing to deal with an old spook like Jacob Stone; facing the Arkwrights of this world is a different matter. Ruthless, he is, and never gives up. Those dogs of his can track prey even across a marsh. Before dawn he'll no doubt catch at least one more of our slimy sisters. But while he's away, we have time to set the first one free!"

With those words Lizzie set off, heading back in the direction we'd come from—toward the old water mill where the spook lived.

When we reached the edge of the moat, Lizzie halted and stared at me hard. "What do I want?" she demanded at last.

"To be carried across the salty water," I replied.

"Of course I do, girl, so what are you waiting for? Shouldn't have to ask, should I? You know what needs to be done!" she hissed.

So I gave Lizzie a piggyback across the moat, through cold water that came just above my knees. Since I wasn't yet a witch, neither the water nor the salt worried me. On the other side, she led the way toward the dilapidated mill. I thought she was going to try and get in through the front door, or maybe break a window. Instead she went around the side, heading toward the waterwheel. There were bits of it missing—it didn't look like it had moved in years, despite the stream that still flowed beneath it.

There was a narrow door beside the wheel, but when Lizzie turned the handle and pushed, she found it was locked.

"Soon have that open," she crowed, bending forward so her mouth was level with the lock. Then she spat into it and muttered a spell I didn't know under her breath. She cocked her head and placed her ear next to it as if listening for something.

Don't know why she needed to put her dirty earhole so close. I heard it from three paces away—the grind and click as the lock opened. With a smile of triumph, Lizzie seized the handle again, turned it, and opened the door.

Inside there was a stink of rotten wood, and the air was damp. It was muddy underfoot, and on our left, through the gloom, I could make out the big curve of the water-wheel. With a mutter, Lizzie tugged something out of her skirt pocket. Instantly a flame flickered into life, and she held it up and led the way forward.

She moved slowly and cautiously. No doubt she reckoned the spook might have set some sort of trap to catch anyone who managed to get inside. She shuffled right and left as if searching for something. Then, at last, she found it.

We came to the edge of a square pit with thirteen bars across the top. Lizzie held out the candle to illuminate it. The pit was filled with water, but there was a shelf of mud on one side, and the captured water witch was lying there on her back, looking up at us, her eyes gleaming in the candlelight.

I'd thought that some of the Pendle witches were ugly, but this water witch was truly grotesque, with her big scary fangs. Would we be safe if Lizzie freed her from the pit? I wondered.

"Listen, sister," Lizzie called down to her. "Come to get you free, we have. In return I've a proposal for you, and another eleven of your kind. Will you take us to your keeper so we can talk terms?"

I wondered what Lizzie meant by "your keeper," but as

usual she didn't bother to explain what was going on.

The witch got to her knees and looked directly at Lizzie. Then I saw her nod.

"Right." Lizzie smirked at me. "We have a deal, girl. I'll soon get her out of here. No time for rats-and-flies magic, so it's lucky we aren't in Chipenden facing one of John Gregory's witch pits. There the bars are securely fixed in place, and without magic we'd need the help of a black-smith to pull 'em free. Here it's just a hinged lid with two locks. Do you know why Arkwright makes it so easy to get in and out of this pit?"

I shrugged. I hadn't got a clue.

"When John Gregory puts a witch in a pit, he means her to stay there until the end of her days, so the bars are permanent. That ain't the case with Arkwright. If a witch kills an adult, it's one year in the pit; two if it's a child. He's like a judge passing sentence, and at the end of their time he pulls 'em out and kills 'em. To make sure they ain't coming back from the dead, he cuts out the heart, slices it in half, and feeds it to his dogs."

Bill Arkwright was a really scary spook. Lizzie's tale made me nervous. What if he tired of the chase and came back? I didn't fancy being shut in one of his slimy pits!

Lizzie spat into each lock, and within moments both had clicked open. The lid was free, but there was no way that she was going to touch it.

"Made of iron, those bars are. You'll have to lift the lid, girl. You ain't a witch yet, so you shouldn't feel much. Get on with it!"

Lizzie might be training me as a witch, but I still had a long way to go yet. So she was right; touching those iron bars didn't hurt at all. The problem was the weight. I struggled for some time before I managed to raise them high enough for Lizzie to kneel at the pit's edge and lean down to offer the water witch her hands.

My whole body was shaking with the effort, but I managed to hold it up long enough for the water witch to be dragged to safety. No sooner was she on the mud floor beside the pit than I let the lid fall back into place with a clang.

Then I stepped back two paces very rapidly. The water witch was crouching, face distorted into a bestial snarl, as if ready to spring at us. She looked hungry for blood rather than grateful for being rescued.

"Right," said Lizzie, who didn't seem in the least perturbed by the witch's attitude. "Let's get clear of here before Arkwright returns with those bog dogs of his. Lead on, sister," she said. "Guide us to somewhere safe."

In reply the water witch merely gave a sort of grimace; it twisted her face so that her mouth opened, revealing more of her sharp yellow teeth. She was covered in slime and dripping with water. She smelled bad, too—the stench of mud, rot, and stagnant ponds. As she walked ahead of us, she waddled slightly. If I hadn't been so nervous, I would have laughed. Water witches weren't suited to land.

We left the mill, and to my surprise, the water witch led us eastward, away from the marsh. We crossed the canal by the nearest bridge and then kept to the hedgerows.

Where could we be going? And how could we ever be safe? Once those wolfhounds got our scent, they'd track us down for sure. Hadn't Lizzie said that Arkwright was relentless and never gave up?

At last, after nearly two hours of scrambling through muddy countryside, the witch pointed across a big field. There was nothing ahead but another distant hedgerow. However, I could sense something . . . something unseen.

But then the witch uttered some disgusting guttural noises and waved her arm about, making signs in the air.

The air shimmered, and suddenly the outline of a building came into view. It had been hidden by magic—some sort of powerful cloaking spell I'd never seen before. As we approached, I saw that it had once been a farmhouse but now seemed deserted. There were no animals in the fields; no dog was set to guard the house. It was in pitch blackness.

Then, by the light of the moon, I saw that there was a large pond beside the house. Most ponds, like middens, were kept some distance away to avoid leakage into the house's cellar. This one had been extended—and in a most unusual way. The water was deep and came right up to the walls of the house, lapping against the brickwork. There was something else strange, too. In what should have been the farmyard sat a huge mound of soil almost as big as the house. It was covered with grass and nettles but didn't look natural. Who had put it there? What was its purpose, and where had the soil come from?

Without looking back at us, the witch slipped into the dark water and disappeared from sight. She was gone a long time, and I wondered if she was gathering some of her sisters to drag us down after her. But then there was a flicker of light from an upstairs window.

"There'll be an entrance under the water," Lizzie said. "No doubt the cellar has been flooded deliberately. But we ain't going in that way. Let's go back to the front door."

Leading the way past the pond, she headed around the side of the house. The glass had gone from the windows, but they had been fixed with board so that you couldn't see inside. The front door looked rotten but was closed. I felt that a good kick with a pointy shoe would shatter it into soggy pieces.

However, we didn't need to do that. I heard the sounds of chains being released and bolts being drawn back, and then the door slowly opened, creaking on its hinges.

A stout, round-faced woman with piggy eyes was standing in the doorway holding up a candle, the better to examine our faces. Her hair was a tangle of gray, and her eyebrows were unkempt; hairs stuck out like a cat's whiskers. She looked anything but friendly.

"What do you want?" she demanded abruptly.

"We rescued one of yours from a pit in the spook's mill," Lizzie said, as if that were all she needed to say to gain entry to the house.

But she was wrong. I didn't like the look of this woman and sensed some threat from her. She wasn't a witch, but she looked very confident as she faced Lizzie. That was unusual. This must be the keeper of the water witches that Lizzie had referred to earlier. I couldn't see why she'd want to live here with all those witches. What did she get out of it?

"Aye, I know that, but what do you want?"

Lizzie forced a smile onto her face. "There's something needs doing, so I want your help to form a coven with those you keep. Just once and for something special. There'll be lots of blood for them, power too. What do you say?"

"What's your name and where be you from?"

"My name is Bony Lizzie, and I'm from Pendle."

"Not much love lost between those from Pendle and those I keep here," the woman replied. "There's been trouble in the past—deaths on both sides."

"You'll get no trouble from me or the girl." Lizzie nodded at me. "Let bygones be bygones, eh? What I propose will be to the benefit of us all. Can't I come inside and talk about it? What's your name—can't you at least tell me who I'm speaking to?"

I thought at first that she was going to refuse, but then she nodded. "My name's Betsy Gammon, and I'll give you just five minutes of my time."

With that, she stood aside, so I followed Lizzie inside. Betsy led us to the rear of the house and into the kitchen. It was dirty, full of rubbish, and there were flies everywhere, most of them disgusting big bluebottles. There was a small door on the right, and she opened it and began to descend some narrow stone steps, her candle sending scary shadows onto the wall. When we reached the cellar, I gazed about me in astonishment.

It was huge, at least three or four times the area of the farmhouse above. At some point, a great deal of excavation had been carried out—the reason, I realized, for the huge pile of soil next to the house. About half the cellar was taken up by a big pit full of water, but on a huge earthen shelf there were several tables and more than twenty stools. In the far corner lay four of those tubular skelt cages. Two of them were occupied. The creatures stared at us with hungry eyes, their long bone tubes jutting out through the bars and quivering with anticipation.

Betsy settled herself down on a stool and stared up at us shrewdly. She didn't invite us to sit. "Well," she said at last, "tell me what your proposal is."

Although the woman wasn't a witch, there was something very threatening about her. She was one of the most horrible people I'd ever met—and that says a lot when you come from a village of Pendle witches as I do.

"Summon twelve of the sisters first," Lizzie said. "I'll put it to all of 'em while you tell me what they say."

Betsy Gammon shook her head. "I don't think you understand what's what here. Not very bright, most of them, are they? So they listen to me and do exactly what I say. They've got the talons and teeth, and I've got the brains." She tapped her head and gave us an evil smile. "So don't waste any more of my time. Explain fully why you're here! It don't do to mess with Betsy!"

Lizzie's face had gone red with anger, and she began to mutter under her breath.

"And don't waste your Pendle spells on me!" Betsy cried. "I've no magic of my own, but I'm shielded by the sisters. Your spells can't hurt me. And all I have to do is whistle, and twenty or more of those I keep will surge up out of that pit and rip you and the girl to shreds. I've half a mind to do it anyway!" She lurched to her feet.

I jumped up in terror, but then Lizzie spoke. "Nay, hear

us out." Her voice was surprisingly gentle, placating the woman. "I didn't know how it was here, but you've put us right. I can see that you run things. Here, let me show you something. . . ."

Lizzie pulled the egg out of her pocket, slowly unfolded the blue silken cloth, and showed it to Betsy. "There's power in this, lots of power!" she exclaimed, eyes bright with excitement. "Stole it from a spook, I did. And a coven could get that power for itself. I'm offering to share it with those you keep."

Betsy scowled at Lizzie, her little piggy eyes almost lost within her bloated face. "Why would you come here when you could share it with your own clan back in Pendle?"

"Had a falling-out with my sisters there," Lizzie lied smoothly. "Almost sent the Malkin assassin after me, they did. Best I stay away until things cool down a bit. That's why I've come to you."

"You're as good as dead if they send Grimalkin after you." Betsy nodded in agreement, her voice softening, too. "So tell me. What needs be done to get that power?"

"It's a full moon three nights from now," said Lizzie. "It has to be done then. We need to sacrifice seven children and drip their blood onto the egg. Then the whole coven performing this rite gets power. Each one of us can make any wish, and it'll come true within seven days!"

Lizzie was crafty, she was. I remembered the exact wording of what the egg had said:

"Give me the heart's blood of seven human children on the night of a full moon. Give me thirteen witches united in that deed, and I will give the one who holds the egg her heart's desire! More power than she has ever dreamed of. Once my need is met, let her think only upon what she wishes, and it will be done within seven days."

Lizzie would be holding the egg, and only *she* would get her wish. The others would be cheated. And to achieve that, seven children would be murdered.

CHAPTER XIII
A Horrible Thing

I knew Lizzie killed people for their bones. I knew she sometimes murdered children—though she'd never done it in front of me before.

There was nothing I could do. If I made a fuss, it would be *my* bones she'd take. She didn't have to spell it out. I knew how it was.

But this was worse than anything that had happened so far.

Seven children were going to be murdered so that Lizzie could get her wish from that evil leather egg. And this time I would be right there in the thick of it.

I'd be as guilty as Lizzie.

I had never wanted to be a witch, but what choice had I been given?

I like to think I was upset on the awful night Lizzie came to claim me, but I don't remember crying. My mam and dad had been cold and dead in the damp earth for three days, and I still hadn't managed to shed a single tear—though it wasn't for want of trying. Tried to remember the good times, I really did. And there were a few, despite the fact that they fought like cat and dog and clouted me harder than they ever hit each other. I mean, you should be upset, shouldn't you? It's your own mam and dad that have just died, so you should be able to squeeze out one tear at least.

It wasn't until much later that I found out that they

weren't my real mam and dad after all. Not only that, they'd been murdered by Lizzie, using a spell that made their blood grow hot and bubble within their veins, so that later it appeared as if they'd just died of a fever. She'd done it so that she could control me and teach me the dark arts.

I had an aunt, Agnes Sowerbutts, and she was kind to me and took me in. But Lizzie wanted me herself, so that was that. The night she came for me there was a bad storm, forks of Fiend lightning sizzling across the sky and crashes of thunder shaking the walls of the cottage and rattling the pots and pans.

But that was nowt compared to what Lizzie did. All day I'd been nervous, waiting for her to come calling, but Agnes had scryed that it would most likely be after dark—Lizzie's favorite time. At last there was a hammering on the door fit to wake the rotting dead, and when Agnes drew back the bolt, Bony Lizzie strode into the room, her black hair matted with rain, water streaming from her cape to cascade onto the stone flags. Poor Agnes was scared, but she stood her ground, bravely placing herself between me and Lizzie.

But I wasn't brave at all. I was terrified—so much so that my knees knocked together and big sobs kept snatching my breath away.

"Leave the girl alone!" Agnes said calmly. "Her home is with me now. She'll be well looked after, don't you worry."

Lizzie's first response was a sneer. They say there's a family resemblance, but I could never have twisted my face the way she did that night. It was enough to turn the milk sour or send the cat shrieking up the chimney as if Old Nick himself were reaching for its tail.

I'd always done my best to keep out of Lizzie's way. It had been over a year since I'd last seen her, and she was scarier than ever. But the day before, news had reached us that she wanted me to live with her. Agnes was supposed to take me to Lizzie's cottage, but I'd pleaded with her not to, and she'd sent word that she wouldn't do it. We'd both known that wouldn't be the end of it.

"The girl belongs to me, Sowerbutts," Lizzie said, her

voice cold and quiet, filled with malice. "We share the same dark blood. I can teach her what she has to know. I'm the one she needs."

I'd known that Lizzie wanted me to live with her but hadn't realized she wanted to train me as a witch. That came as a real shock.

I remember thinking that she was just about the *last* thing I needed, but as I said, I was really scared and kept my mouth shut.

"Alice needn't be a witch like you!" Agnes retorted. "Her mam and dad weren't witches, so why should she follow your dark path? Leave her be. Leave the girl with me and go about your business."

"She's the blood of a witch inside her and that's enough!" Lizzie hissed angrily. "You're just an outsider and not fit to raise the girl."

It wasn't true. Agnes was a Deane, all right, but she'd married a good honest man from Whalley, an ironmonger. When he'd died, she'd returned to Roughlee, where the Deane witch clan made its home.

"I'm her aunt, and I'll be a mother to her now," Agnes said. She still spoke bravely, but her face was pale, and I could see her plump chin wobbling, her hands fluttering and trembling with fear.

By now I'd edged away into the far corner of the room, wondering if I could slip away into the kitchen, reach the back door, and make a run for it. I knew that the argument between Lizzie and Agnes wouldn't last long. I knew who'd win.

Next thing, Lizzie stamped her left foot. It was as easy as that. In the twinkling of an eye, the fire died in the grate, the candles flickered and went out, and the whole room became instantly dark, cold, and terrifying. I heard Agnes cry out in terror, and I was screaming myself, desperate to flee. I would have run through the closed door, jumped through a window, or even scrabbled my way up the chimney. I'd have done anything just to escape.

But I couldn't move a muscle. I was paralyzed with fear.

I did get out, but with Lizzie at my side. She just seized me by the wrist and dragged me off into the night. It was no use trying to resist—she was too strong and held me tight, her nails digging into my skin. I belonged to her now, and there was no way she was ever going to let me go. And that night she began my training as a witch. It was the start of all my troubles.

That was how it had begun with Lizzie, and my training had indeed been hard and unpleasant.

With the murder of seven children it was going to get a whole lot worse.

I was about to take the first proper step toward becoming a malevolent witch. If I helped Lizzie with this, there would be no going back.

Betsy put two fingers in her mouth and gave a piercing shriek. It was enough to make your ears bleed. Something surged up out of the water and landed on its feet on the soft ground facing her. Muddy water went everywhere, and I took a quick step backward.

It was a water witch, wearing rags covered in green and brown scum, her hair matted, face filthy with muck. I'd seen those murderous talons before, but what I hadn't noticed was the deadly feet. The witch had webbed toes, each one ending in a sharp talon. I guessed they would propel her fast through the water; she could fight, cut, and kill with all four limbs.

Betsy Gammon began to talk to her in the language of the water witches. Most of it was made up of grunts and other noises—something between a bark and an old tomcat spitting up a hairball. But there were a few words I recognized: "blood" and "skelt" were two that I would have expected to be part of the conversation between a water witch and her keeper, and both were uttered several times.

I also heard the name Arkwright, which didn't surprise me. The local spook must be an ever-present danger to these witches. He hunted them down with his two fearsome dogs and kept them away from the monastery ruins, a place that was sacred to them. There was also the considerable danger that he would one day discover the whereabouts of this farm and put an end to their keeper, scattering the witches and making their activities as a coven more difficult. They must be using powerful magic to cloak the building and keep the dogs from following the scent of a witch here. But how long could they keep that up? The use of magic could be very taxing; it must require a good deal of blood.

In reply to Betsy's long monologue, the water witch gave just a single grunt before turning and diving back into the water with hardly a splash. She didn't even look at us. When she had disappeared, the keeper turned to confront Lizzie again.

"It will be done," she said. "But first we need children. It's best to have more than seven. Extras always come in useful—skelts love their sweet young blood. They must be taken from the east, well away from the local spook's territory. We will supply twelve brats. You must bring us the thirteenth. We all contribute. Isn't that fair?"

I shuddered, but Lizzie agreed. "Aye, that's very fair. I'll do my share."

"Then be back here one night before the full moon and bring your sacrifice! But first I'll cook you some supper.

It's best to dine together to seal a bargain."

I didn't fancy eating anything out of that dirty kitchen, but I didn't have much choice, did I?

"Gammon by name and gammon's what I love to eat!" Betsy cackled as if this were a great joke, then bade us sit at the grimy table and handed out plates.

She'd cooked the gammon so that it melted in my mouth. The problem was, it immediately sent me into a coughing fit. Gammon is always on the salty side, but this was almost inedible, and I found myself choking.

Lizzie nibbled a little, trying to hide her annoyance at being given salty gammon. Then I saw her slyly spit it out under the table when Betsy wasn't looking. Witches had an aversion to salt. Even in food, it could be dangerous. Betsy knew that only too well and was enjoying Lizzie's discomfort.

Betsy herself was no witch. There was a small pot of salt on the table, and she kept dipping her fingers into it and licking them with relish.

After a while Lizzie commented on it. "You certainly

like a bit of salt with your food, Betsy," she said with an ingratiating smile.

"Aye, that I do," she replied. "That's why some call me Salty Betsy!"

Lizzie and Betsy had a good old cackle over that, but once they'd calmed down, Betsy became serious.

"I don't have any magic of my own, you see. Nothing to keep 'em at bay. And the slimy sisters can be funny at times. It's bloodlust that does it. They can turn on you in an instant. But salt discourages them. So I eat lots of it. Smear it in my hair, too. It works a treat!"

With that meal, the contract was sealed, and leaving Betsy still stuffing salty gammon into her mouth, I followed Lizzie out the door into the chilly night air.

Lizzie looked up at the moon and faint stars, and then did a slow circle, her eyes sweeping the house, nearby trees, and the distant horizon to the west.

"Just fixing this place in my head, girl," she told me with a smirk. "Wouldn't do to catch our brat an' not be able to find it again."

We hadn't gone more than fifty paces east before the old farmhouse, its pond and big mound of dirt all disappeared from view, cloaked again by dark magic.

We covered about a dozen miles before dawn, and then settled down to hide for the daylight hours in a small copse. We were less than two miles from a village, and there were lights showing from a couple of farmhouses ahead, the farmers already up and beginning their predawn chores.

"I'm famished, girl! Get us some rabbits!" Lizzie snapped.

I was still hungry too, not having been able to eat more than a mouthful of that salty gammon. So I caught, skinned, and gutted a couple of rabbits and cooked them on the smallest fire I could manage. It was no more than embers when the tip of the sun peered above the horizon. We didn't want smoke to give away our position.

Stomachs full, we settled down to sleep. I was still thinking about everything that had happened over the past few days, but Lizzie was very soon lying on her back, mouth wide open, snoring away. Occasionally she muttered in her sleep and a smile split her face. She was dreaming, probably about her clever scheme to fool the water witches and their keeper and have the power of the leather egg all to herself. But I couldn't sleep, no matter how hard I tried.

I couldn't stop thinking about what we were planning to do. When night fell, Lizzie would target one of the outlying village houses and snatch a child. And that child would die—either as part of the ritual or to be drained by a skelt.

I would be a murderer, too.

Lizzie managed to sleep right through the day until the sun went down. The moment the light began to fail, she sat up, stretched, yawned, and spat into the cold gray embers of the fire.

"Well, girl, let's get on with it," she said, clambering to her feet.

I followed her out of the trees, and keeping to the shelter of a hedgerow, we approached the nearer of two farms.

Lizzie paused and sniffed three times. "Nowt there!" she exclaimed. "No young bones, just a skinny old farmer and his fat, stinky sow of a wife. And they've got big dogs, too!"

No sooner had she spoken than they began to bark, and Lizzie moved on quickly, keeping her distance from the threat.

We headed northeast, approaching the village at a tangent. It was dark now, and the moon had yet to rise, but there were lights showing from the bedroom windows of one of the houses. It was set some distance from the others, and Lizzie made a beeline for it.

This time, after pausing to sniff, she gave a cackle of delight. "Just a woman and her brat of a daughter, so it couldn't be better!" she crowed. "No dog, either."

She led the way to the front door. I could just make out the shape of a cat on the step.

The poor animal made two mistakes. First, it hissed at Lizzie. That was bad enough. But when she tried to sweep it off the step with the back of her hand, it scratched and hung on to her, its claws embedded in her flesh.

Faster than a snake striking, Lizzie picked it up and, holding it with two hands, twisted the animal violently. I heard a sound like a twig snapping underfoot. She flung the body away into a clump of nettles. Then she knelt and spat into the lock.

Moments later the lock clicked, and Lizzie eased the door open. She stepped inside and turned to face me. "Wait at the bottom of the stairs. If anybody gets past me, don't let them out of the house, understand?"

I nodded, though my heart was pounding, and watched Lizzie climb slowly up toward the bedroom. It was dark inside the house—the bedroom lights were off now—and she disappeared into the gloom at the top. I heard her open a door, and then, suddenly, a child began to scream in terror. The cries quickly gave way to a shrill, frantic pleading.

"Mam! Mam! Help me, please! A horrible thing is here. It's got me. Help me! Help me, Mam!"

One part of me felt sorry for the child and wanted to help her. I couldn't help putting myself in her place and experiencing the terror of being snatched by a witch in the middle of the night. But there was nothing I could do.

I heard another door open, and then heavy footsteps.

The mother was awake and rushing toward her daughter. But what chance did she have against a witch such as Bony Lizzie?

There was another terrible scream, this time from the woman, followed by a heavy thump.

"You've killed Mam!" the child cried out. "Oh, Mam! Mam! My poor mam!"

Lizzie had murdered the mother! And in front of her own daughter, too! I felt sick to my stomach.

CHAPTER XIV
WHAT CAN YOU DO?

"**Y**OU'LL be next if you don't shut your stinking gob!" Lizzie cried, and I heard her clumping down the stairs toward me.

She pushed past, carrying the child, who was sobbing pitifully. She was a skinny little thing, no older than six. I suddenly felt angry. I raced after Lizzie, grabbed her arm, and brought her to a halt. She spun around to face me, eyes wild with anger.

"Why did you have to murder her mother?" I demanded. "Ain't the rest of it bad enough without that?"

Lizzie glared at me. Had her hands been free, she'd have slapped me hard for sure. I was shaking with fear at what I'd just done—grabbing her arm and shouting at her like that. True, we'd had words before, but I'd never been so openly defiant.

"Know your place, girl, or you'll be sorry!" she warned, her mouth twitching dangerously, showing how close she was to hurting me. "I just used a sleep-now spell on her. Her mam shouldn't be dead, not unless she broke her silly neck when she fell. And that would serve her right for being so fat!"

With that, she strode off westward, into the dark, carrying the sobbing child.

I really wanted to help that little girl. But what could I do against Lizzie's magic? If she stopped to sleep or rest, I might get a chance to try something, but it would be risky;

I'd pay a terrible price if I was caught. I was probably wasting my time even thinking about it, because I knew she wouldn't stop until we reached the water witches' lair.

By morning there'd be a hue and cry—that was, if the mother did recover from the effects of Lizzie's spell. If she had broken her neck, it might be hours or even days before neighbors found her body and realized that the girl was missing. But no doubt the witches were grabbing other children right now, and the hunt for the abductors would begin. Every able-bodied person for miles would be up in arms. Despite the distance from the mill, they'd finally alert the spook, Arkwright. His dogs and eyes might be baffled by the cloaking magic, but this whole area would be searched. I knew Lizzie wanted to reach that refuge as quickly as possible.

We got back well before dawn and found that the cloaking of the farm was still of the highest standard. Lizzie sniffed and cursed, studying the stars and the horizon in frustration for nearly an hour. I hoped she might hand the girl to me—I could pretend to stumble and allow her to make a run for it. But Lizzie kept a fierce grip on her prize every second of the way. Finally she backtracked and led us to a place where the air shimmered to reveal the house.

Betsy was waiting at the open door, and she grinned and beckoned us inside. As we followed her down the cellar steps, I heard the cries. The child Lizzie carried was still sobbing, but this was a loud wail from more than one child . . . a cacophony of misery.

The sight that greeted me in that gloomy cellar made me sick to my stomach. There were more than a dozen new cages now—larger ones, intended to hold children rather than skelts. Four of these had occupants; one was asleep, three crying their lungs out with fear. All were covered in slime, and one, a little boy with two front teeth missing, was dripping wet.

There were more confined skelts than last time, too—six of them now, all staring out at the children and twitching with hunger.

"Give her to me!" Betsy Gammon demanded, and Lizzie handed the little girl over without question. The huge woman lifted her up and held her at arm's length. "A skinny little thing, but better than nowt! We'll need to feed her up!" she declared, before thrusting her into a cage and clicking a lock into place.

"We're still two short of the seven we require," Lizzie said, "but I've kept my end of the bargain."

"That you have," Betsy agreed. "But don't worry. Tomorrow night a bunch of my girls will be on their way to a place where there should be rich pickings. It's an orphanage run by a few scrawny old nuns. So soon we should have brats to spare!"

The next couple of days became a nightmare. Lizzie and Betsy were getting on like a house on fire now, cackling together in an upstairs room and sipping dandelion wine. While they did that, I was given all the chores to do, the worst being to look after the children they'd stolen.

I didn't want to face them, didn't want to be confronted by their misery . . . but someone had to do it. They needed to be fed and kept alive until the ritual at the full moon.

Lizzie would have been happy for me to push stale bread through the bars of their cage and tip a cupful of water into each little mouth.

However, I couldn't leave them sitting there in their own stink, so I dealt with them one at a time, opening each cage to let them out to be fed and cleaned up.

One night Lizzie caught me asking one little girl her name. I was just trying to be friendly and make the child feel a little better, but Lizzie scoffed at me.

"You're a fool, girl!" she hissed into my ear, giving the child a false smile. "Why waste your time learning her name when she'll be dead soon? You'd be better off studying your spells."

But once Lizzie had gone, I carried on as before. I also gave each child ten minutes to walk about and stretch their legs a bit. Most sniffled and sobbed and stared at the caged skelts openmouthed, clearly terrified of the creatures.

Just a few hours before midnight, when they were due to be sacrificed, I was cleaning up the little girl that Lizzie had snatched. She didn't stop talking, and her words were painful to hear: "Mam's dead! She killed her. Struck her down dead!" she wailed.

"She ain't dead." I tried to make my voice as soft and reassuring as possible. "It was just a spell to make her sleep. By now she'll have woken up. So don't you worry. Your mam's all right."

"She hit her head when she fell. Made a big thump. Blood trickled out of her ear. I saw it."

"She'll recover. Your mam is strong. It'll take more than a bump on the head to finish her off," I insisted, taking her hand.

Despite my reassuring words, I began to wonder if the girl's mother might actually be dead. I didn't like what she'd said about blood trickling out of her ear. Back in Pendle I'd once watched a boy climb a big tree, cheered on by his friends. He'd climbed too high, onto a thin branch that wouldn't bear his weight. It had snapped, and he'd plunged to the ground and hit his head on a rock. He'd bled from both ears and never woke up. They carried him home, and I heard he'd died soon afterward.

"But what if Mam's hurt and can't walk? She might die of thirst without help. She might be dying now!"

With that, the little girl tore her hand free of mine and ran toward the door. I managed to catch her before she reached the top of the steps. Good thing I did, or there'd have been hell to pay. I carried her kicking and screaming back to her cage, locked her inside, and was forced to feed her through the bars.

"What's your name?" I asked when she'd finally calmed down.

"Emily. My name's Emily Jenks," she replied with a sniff.

"Well, Emily, there's no need to worry. Your mam will be fine."

"Will I ever see her again?"

"Of course you will."

"Maybe it'd be better if Mam was dead," Emily said softly.

"Why do you say that?" I asked.

"Because then I will see her again. We'll be together again when we're both dead."

"Don't be silly, you're just a child. It'll be a long time before you die," I lied.

"That isn't what the fat lady said. She said we'd be given to those horrible things!" Emily cried, pointing through the bars toward the nearest skelt cage. The occupant was staring at us with evident interest. "She said it would stick its long, sharp snout into us and suck up our blood until our hearts stopped beating."

Some of the nearer children heard that and started crying. I was appalled. The children were scared enough as it was. Why make it worse by telling them they were going to die in such a horrible way?

What kind of a monster *was* Betsy Gammon? In some ways she was far worse than the witches she kept. Without her, the killing would be random and less frequent. She organized the water witches and made the slaying of innocents happen on a bigger scale. Of course, this time Lizzie had started it, seeking the power of that egg.

"Look . . . that's not going to happen," I said, hoping one of the cackling hags from upstairs didn't suddenly decide to pay the children a visit. "She's just trying to scare you."

"Then why did you steal me from my mam and bring me here? And why are those creatures in the cages staring at us all the time? Are they hungry? Do they want our blood?" Emily cried.

I was just as guilty as Lizzie. "Don't worry, they ain't going to get your blood," I said.

"But the fat lady said they would."

"It ain't true. I won't let that happen."

"You're only a girl. What can you do? The witches are fierce, with big teeth and claws, and there's lots and lots of 'em!"

I thought for a moment before answering. Up until now I'd just tried to be cheerful and optimistic, to give the child some hope. Then words just flowed from my mouth as if my answer had come from somebody else.

"I'm Alice, and I won't let them hurt you. I can stop them. I *can* and I *will*!"

I must have said it with real conviction, because the girl's eyes widened and her mouth dropped open in astonishment. For the first time she seemed calm.

My business in the cellar finished, I walked back up the steps to ground level. I heard Lizzie and Betsy still chatting and laughing together upstairs. I couldn't bear the sight of either of them, so I walked out into the yard and stared at the pond for a while, thinking things through.

How foolish I'd been to claim that I could prevent the child from being hurt. What could I actually do? I wondered.

Nothing! Nothing at all!

No, that wasn't quite true. Within hours those children would all be dead, but I could do something for myself. I could run away from this terrible place so that when they died I would no longer be here. I wouldn't be a murderer, then.

Not only that—I could escape from Lizzie. That way I wouldn't have to become a witch.

But how badly would she want me back? Last time

she'd known I was staying with Agnes Sowerbutts. And Agnes hadn't been strong enough to protect me from such a strong malevolent witch. But this time I could flee far from Pendle, and Lizzie wouldn't know where. Even if she managed to scry my whereabouts, she'd be too busy wielding the power from that leather egg to bother her head about me.

So why waste time? Better to go now, this very minute.

CHAPTER XV
Elizabeth of the Bones

WITHOUT a backward glance,
I left the yard and walked east, back in
the direction of the canal. I intended to
follow it south, but I wouldn't be heading toward Pendle. I'd keep going until
I was far beyond the County. They
said the weather was warmer down
south and that it didn't rain as much. It
would be good to get a bit more sun on

my face. I hated this damp, blustery County climate.

The light was beginning to fail, so the sun must be very close to the horizon. Not that there was much chance of seeing it. Low gray clouds were rushing in from the west. Soon it would rain.

I felt no lifting of my spirits, no happiness at the thought that I was leaving my old life forever. In my chest, where my heart should have been, was a lump of cold lead that made it difficult to breathe. I kept seeing the hungry skelts and those frightened children in their cages. Seven of them would be sacrificed in order to release the power of the egg; the remainder would be given to those bloodthirsty creatures.

The farther I walked, the worse I felt. Even if I were many miles away when they killed those children, I'd still be guilty, wouldn't I?

I'd kept watch while Lizzie snatched the child and hurt—maybe even killed—the mother. There was more than one type of guilt. You might do something horrible that you later regretted. But you could also feel guilty for something that you'd *not* done! If I didn't help the children in some way, that guilt would stay with me for the rest of my life.

Something struck me like lightning. I could go and tell Arkwright, the spook, and lead him to the children. I could take him through the magical cloak, straight to the house.

But that would be very risky. He might assume that I was a witch, and either put me in a pit or kill me on sight! Still, it was a chance. I might be able to persuade him of the danger that faced the children; and I was the only one who could lead him through the magic cloak to save them. . . .

Once there, I could slip away while he sorted out the witches and that pig Salty Betsy. No doubt Lizzie would get away; she was crafty and had more lives than a cat.

Yes, that's what I would do, I thought. So I pressed on faster toward the canal. Once I reached it, the mill lay only a little way farther north.

I couldn't have been more than five minutes from the canal when it began to rain really hard—the kind of downpour that could soak you to the skin in minutes. Next forked lightning suddenly split the sky, to be followed moments later by a loud thunderclap almost directly overhead. It reminded me of that bad storm the night Lizzie had snatched me from Agnes's house.

I've always been afraid of being struck by lightning. It scares me almost as much as spiders and flies. The Malkin coven was once caught in a bad storm on Pendle Hill. One of 'em was struck dead on the spot. And when they carried her corpse back to the village, it was all blackened and burned. It happened before I was born, but they say the stink of her charred body hung in the air for weeks afterward.

Where could I shelter? There were a few isolated trees, but it was dangerous to take refuge beneath them, and the nearby hedgerow wouldn't keep me dry for long, or safe from the lightning.

It was almost dark, and in the distance I now saw a faint light—it seemed to come from south of the canal. That probably meant a farm. Perhaps I could shelter in one of the outbuildings. No doubt there'd be dogs. They'd get my scent and bark fit to wake the dead, but the farmer wasn't likely to venture out in such filthy weather after dark.

So I began to walk faster, cutting across two big fields and climbing over a gate, all the while making directly for that light.

Because of the cloud cover, there was neither moon nor stars to light my way, and the rain was driving horizontally into my face now, making it hard to see much. So it wasn't until I got much closer to the light that I realized my mistake.

Its source wasn't a farmhouse window or a lantern hanging from a barn door.

It was a barge moored on the canal.

I halted on the towpath and stared at it. It was big, black, and shiny, a far cry from the working craft that usually plied the canal, carrying food, coal, and other materials between Caster and Kendal. It had a flat deck and one closed hatch.

Then I looked at the source of the light that had drawn

me across the fields like a foolish moth to the flame that would consume it. On the prow stood thirteen large black candles. They burned steadily, without even the slightest flicker, despite the gusts of wind that snatched the breath from my open mouth. It was still raining hard, churning up the surface of the canal, but not one drop reached the deck of that mysterious barge.

The candles bothered me. Black ones were used by witches—they made me think of the dark. But the barge was very grand and beautiful, which made me put aside most of my fears.

I was rooted to the spot, unable to tear my gaze from the candles and run away. Then, out of the corner of my eye, I noticed a movement. I finally turned and saw that the hatch was slowly sliding open.

I gasped in astonishment at what was revealed. There were steps leading downward—too many steps. Canals were not deep, so barges were flat bottomed. These steps went down too far. It was impossible, yet I could see them there in front of me.

Anyone with a shred of common sense would have turned and fled. But I wasn't thinking straight. I felt compelled to step onto the deck of that black barge and go down into that deep hold. And that's what I did, as if walking in a dream.

A dream? Looking back, it was a nightmare!

Apart from dozens of candles positioned in clusters, there was just one object in that big hold: a large throne of dark, shiny wood. It was covered in carvings of evil-looking creatures—dragons, snakes, and all sorts of monstrosities. But the throne was unoccupied; there was no one else in the hold . . . at least, nobody I could see. The hairs on the back of my neck began to stand up, and I felt as if someone was watching me. Nevertheless, I walked forward and stood facing the empty throne.

Who would sit on a throne like that, anyway?

I hadn't spoken those words aloud, but immediately I got an answer to my question.

"A good friend of yours would sit on that throne if he could, Alice. I am that friend. One day, with your help, that may be possible."

I was confused. I didn't have any good friends. The words had come from some distance behind the throne. It was a young voice, that of a boy.

"How do you know my name?" I asked.

"I know your name as well as your predicament, Alice. I know that you serve Elizabeth of the Bones unwillingly, and you fear what she might soon do to a number of poor innocent children."

I had never heard her referred to by that name, but I knew he meant Bony Lizzie.

"Who are you? And how do you know so much about me?" I asked nervously. I noticed that whereas the candle flames on the deck had burned steadily despite the storm, here in the perfect calm of the hold they flickered wildly, as if in response to some ghostly wind.

"I am an unseen prince of this world, and it is my duty to know all about my subjects. I can help you, Alice. All you need to do is ask."

"Where are you now? Could I see you?"

"I am far away, but you may see my image for a moment. Look just directly above the throne. But don't blink—it cannot stay here long!"

As bidden, I looked at a point just above that shiny ebony throne. For a moment nothing happened, but then there was a shimmer, and a face, without a body, appeared before me.

It was the face of a boy of about thirteen or fourteen, barely older than me. He wore a broad smile, and his hair was a mass of golden curls that gleamed in the candlelight. He was good to look at; it was clear that he would grow up to become a very handsome young man. Not only that. Kindness and friendship beamed out at me. I felt as if he really cared what happened to me, as if he would do anything he could to help me. No one had ever cared much for me—apart from Agnes, maybe. My mam and dad had been cruel to me, and I hadn't seen much of Agnes anyway. So it warmed my heart to see someone looking at me like that. I felt that my life might begin properly if he was my friend.

"Would you help me, please?" I found myself saying. All fear and nervousness had left me. I felt happy and sure that somehow things would turn out for the best. "I want to help those children. I was on my way to see Arkwright, the spook, and take him to the house where the children are held captive."

"You needn't waste your time going to get the aid of a spook," he replied as his image faded and vanished. *"Look inside yourself. You have the strength and power to do whatever you wish! You need no one but yourself!"*

I thought back to the testing in Pendle, the time when a young potential witch is tested to see what her strengths are and what type of magic she should use. Mine had been a terrifying experience that had gone badly. But I had learned from it that I might one day become very powerful. Now I was hearing it again. Could I start to believe it?

"What can I do against all those fierce witches?" I asked. "Lizzie alone would sort me out proper in seconds. She's forgotten more spells than I've managed to learn so far. And what about the sharp teeth and claws of the others? What have I got to match that?"

"Match it? You can surpass it with ease. As I said, the power is

within you. Look for it now! Search within yourself!" continued the disembodied voice.

"How can I do that?" I asked.

"Begin by closing your eyes," the voice said softly.

I obeyed, eager to learn. Wouldn't it be wonderful to be powerful and not spend my life being scared? I thought.

I could see the light flickering through the blood within my eyelids.

"Relax and drift downward!" commanded the voice. *"Go down into the darkness, deep within yourself."*

For a moment I fought that instruction. The thought of going down into darkness was scary. But I was already moving; it was too late. I sank slowly at first, then faster and faster. I left my stomach behind and fell, like a stone kicked into an abyss, anticipating some fearful impact when I reached the bottom. I was terrified. I was lost and about to be destroyed. Why had I listened to this boy?

But there was no blow, no collision. Instead I found myself floating in darkness, utterly at peace. And suddenly I discovered the power that the handsome boy had spoken of. It was inside me, part of me; something I owned. It was something that I had been born with. Until this moment I had not been aware that I possessed such strength. Before I'd felt vulnerable, prone to being pushed and hurt by those around me. Now I had no doubt that I had the strength to push back.

"See? You don't need spells, Alice, but speak them if they make you comfortable. All you need do is focus your mind and exert your will! Wish for what you want. Say to yourself, 'I am Alice.' Then be Alice. Nothing can then stand against you. Do you believe me?"

"Yes! Yes, I do!" I cried. It was true. I had absolute faith in what the voice promised. When I'd promised little Emily that I would stop her from being harmed, the words had come out of me without prior thought. And I'd really believed what I said to her. Perhaps that was because, deep down, a part of me already *knew* that I possessed the power to make it happen.

"Then go in peace, and do what must be done in order to save those poor children. One day we will meet again, and then you will be able to help me."

One second I was drifting happily in absolute darkness; the next I was standing on the canal towpath in the rain, with the thunder rumbling overhead.

The barge had vanished.

Without hesitation, filled with a terrible certainty that I could intervene and rescue those children from the witches, I set off east toward the house of Salty Betsy.

I walked fast—but would I be too late?

CHAPTER XVI
THE DANCE OF DEATH

I was dripping wet by the time I was even halfway there, my hair soaked and my pointy shoes squelching in the soggy grass. And as I walked, the confidence and determination that had come to me on the canal slowly ebbed away.

Now the barge and its strange occupant seemed nothing but a dream.

Had it really happened? If so, what I'd believed at the time now seemed foolish. Lizzie was a really strong malevolent witch. I thought of the sprogs that she could summon from the dark to torment me. They usually just scratched and nipped a bit, but the threat of worse was always there. One had once pushed itself into my left nostril. If I hadn't screamed for mercy to make Lizzie relent, it might have crawled right up into my brain and started to feed. Could I really disobey her? I wondered.

There were no stars visible, so I wasn't sure of the time, but it had to be approaching midnight. I walked even faster, finally breaking into a run.

Where was the house? It must be close by now. Then I remembered how difficult it had been even for Lizzie to find it. And she had studied the horizon in order to note its position. I had done the same, but it had been daylight then; now it was night, and the low cloud and rain obscured everything. Not only that, the magic cloaking it was very strong.

I became desperate. By now the witches might have

already begun to kill the children. Where was the house?

Show yourself! I thought desperately. *Show yourself!*

And suddenly, lit by a flash of lightning, the house appeared.

It wasn't as if I had gotten lucky and blundered through the cloak by chance. Because of the rain and poor visibility, like a small boat battling a storm, I had drifted off course. It was about two hundred strides to my left. I had been about to pass right by it.

Had I somehow broken through that powerful magical cloak with my will? Had I drawn upon the magic deep within me without even muttering a spell, just as the boy on the barge had told me I could?

I turned and began to run toward the house. Perhaps I wasn't too late, after all . . . ? But what would I do when I got there?

With its boarded-up windows, the house appeared to be in darkness, barely an outline against the clouds. But I knew that down in the cellar, flickering candles and torches would be illuminating a scene of horror.

Lightning flashed again almost directly overhead, showing the surface of the pond churning under the force of the rain, which hammered down on the roof and cascaded in sheets from the overburdened gutters.

I reached the front door and tried the handle. It turned, but the door resisted my pressure. They had locked it. I bent forward, preparing to spit into the lock and use the spell of opening. Lizzie had mastered it, but my grasp of it was less sure. I hadn't used it by myself before. But then I remembered what the boy aboard the barge had said:

"You don't need spells, Alice, but speak them if they make you comfortable. All you need do is focus your mind and exert your will! Wish for what you want. Say to yourself, 'I am Alice.' Then be Alice. Nothing can then stand against you. Do you believe me?"

The house had revealed itself in response to my command. So I straightened my back, looked down at the lock, and concentrated.

"Open!" I commanded.

There was a click, and in obedience to my wish, the lock turned. I liked that. It made me feel in control. It made me believe that perhaps I *could* rescue those children, despite the great odds against me.

I eased open the door and went inside, closing it softly behind me. It was dark within, but I remembered the way to the cellar steps. I waited for a moment before going down, my sense of urgency temporarily overwhelmed by the new wave of fear that washed over me.

But the sounds I heard from below spurred my feet to begin a rapid descent. There were wails of fear; a child screamed as if within an inch of losing its life.

When I reached the foot of the stone steps, I waited for a second or two, taking in the scene before me. It seemed that the water witches had decided to begin by gathering blood from the skelts in order to increase their power. Seven of the children were still in their cages. They must be the ones chosen for the ritual with Jacob Stone's egg later. Six others were already staked out on the cellar floor; a skelt was being released from its cage even as I watched.

Some of the water witches were gathered around the terrified children. I counted them quickly, noting their positions; there were twelve, making Lizzie the thirteenth member of the temporary coven. She was sitting on a stool, clutching the leather egg to her bosom, a self-satisfied smile on her face. Other witches were in the water, clearly enjoying the proceedings. Some surged up like excited seals, only to dive back in with hardly a ripple. Nobody seemed to be looking in my direction.

But where was Salty Betsy? There was no sign of her.

I had taken everything in with little more than a glance. I felt sharp and alert. Now I noticed that the skelt was advancing toward one of the children. It scuttled forward, its multijointed legs a blur, bone tube raised, ready to plunge into the neck of its first screaming victim.

I had to do something quickly. . . .

Rage and revulsion fill me.

I concentrate.

Stare hard at the advancing creature.

I will it away from the child. Push it with my mind.

It is thrown backward, high into the air, as if seized by

an invisible giant hand. It halts impossibly close to the ceiling, floats there as if time is freezing, then is hurled violently against the far wall of the cellar.

The skelt splatters against the stones, its head breaking with a loud crack. It slithers down like a squashed bug, leaving a slimy trail of blood and brains. Then it enters the water with a loud splash and quickly sinks from sight.

There is a moment's silence.

The children stop crying; the screaming pauses.

All the witches turn to look at me, hatred and anger etched on their faces.

It is Lizzie who attacks first. Clutching the egg in her right hand, she runs toward me, the fingers of her other hand extended as if she means to scratch out my eyes.

I wait calmly, taking in a deep, slow breath.

I am not afraid.

I am Alice.

I step aside, and Lizzie's hand misses my face. I extend my foot. She trips over it, falling headlong onto the muddy floor of the cellar. The leather egg spills from her grasp and rolls away, right to the edge of the water.

The children are silent.

It is the witches who scream now. They scream in rage.

I look down at Lizzie, who is sprawled in the mud. She glares up at me with hatred. Her mouth twists in a sneer.

She is still a threat, and I will have to deal with her very soon.

But it is the water witches who pose the more immediate danger. Wild with anger, they run at me, all fangs and claws. They have tremendous strength. They could rip me limb from limb, devour my flesh, drink my blood, and chew my bones into fragments.

They could. But I will not allow it.

I have no talons of my own. My teeth are ordinary teeth. I have no blades at my disposal.

I have only my magic.

And there is more than one way to use it.

I wish I had the abilities of another—someone more capable of dealing with this threat.

I slip off my pointy shoes and grip one in each hand.

Their heels will be my weapons. All I need is the skill. So I wield my magic and gather it to me. I exert my will. Now I have the innate ability and honed skill of the greatest warrior. I feel it pour into my body.

I am Alice.

The first of the water witches reaches for me. I step aside and clout her hard with the heel of my pointy shoe. She goes down. She now has a third eye in her forehead; a red one, dribbling blood.

I spin and whirl, doing the dance of Grimalkin; the dance of death. And I strike left, right, and left again. Each savage strike makes contact. Each blow fells an enemy. And I wish them to be terrified. That is my will.

Soon they are fleeing.

Some splash into the water and escape that way. Others scamper up the steps.

I feel so strong. Even the threat of Morwena does not concern me. Let her come. I will deal with her, too!

But Morwena does not show herself. It is almost a disappointment.

Now only Lizzie remains.

She scrambles to her feet, daubed in mud.

The moment of reckoning has arrived.

Something inside me wants to kill her. She is a murderess—a slayer of innocent children. The world would be a much better place without her. I gather my will, but then I hesitate. I cannot do it.

She is family. I will not take her life.

Then I remember what she did to me, and I smile.

The sprogs! I will use the sprogs to torment her!

Can I do that? Will they obey my command? Is my magic that strong?

Using my will, I summon them from the dark. Full of hunger, they surge into our world.

I hurl them at Lizzie.

When I leave with the children, she is in serious trouble.

She is screaming.

One sprog is already forcing itself into her ear. She is fighting desperately, vainly. Another is scratching its way up into her left nostril. So I put a limit on things. Give it five minutes before the sprogs go back to the dark.

Next I look over to where the egg is balanced on the edge of the muddy shelf. I walk toward it. But then something strange occurs. Something writhes upward; a long, thin multijointed limb.

I recognize it immediately.

It is the foreleg of a skelt. One must have been lurking in the water. The limb moves toward the leather egg.

I step forward to seize it. It should be kept safe, far from Lizzie's clutches.

But then I halt and relax.

Let the skelt take it. It will be safer beyond Lizzie's reach.

However . . . I consider the water witches who might still be able to locate and retrieve it.

I have hesitated too long.

The limb grips the leather egg and draws it down beneath the surface with hardly more than a ripple. It is a strange thing for the skelt to do. Why does it want the egg? I push it from my mind. The children must be returned to their homes.

❂ ❂ ❂

As I led the way out of the house, I realized it was still raining. But the children didn't seem to care. When I looked
back at them, I saw that most were chatting excitedly, just
glad to be away from the witches and scary skelts.

Some would be going home to their families, others to
the orphanage. I wondered if they were happy there.

Then I noticed Emily, the girl whose mother Lizzie had
attacked. She was not talking to anyone. I made up my
mind to go back, take her by the hand, and ask her to walk
alongside me. But suddenly I was distracted.

As we passed the pond, a figure stepped out of the shadows and ran toward me. The children scattered, but I
stood my ground.

It was Betsy Gammon.

"You've spoiled things for me, girl!" she said, spitting her
words out in a fury, her piggy eyes almost popping from
her head. "I can't use magic, but that was my one chance to
have that kind of power. You've taken it from me!"

She had a long, curved blade in her right hand, and I

had no doubt that she intended to kill me. She was almost within striking range. Death was in her eyes, so I defended myself instinctively. Using magic, I pushed her away from me.

She flew back, up into the air, head over heels, and dropped into the pond with a loud splash.

Moments later she came to the surface, spluttering and gasping. She began to flail her arms, and her face was filled with panic.

I realized that she couldn't swim.

It was strange to think that she was a keeper of water witches and that their natural environment could be her death. I felt torn. I could use my magic again to save her. But what would I be saving her for? So that she could organize her witches again? So that other children would die?

In anguish, pulled between actions and inaction, I did nothing. We watched in silence from the bank while she struggled and finally sank from sight.

CHAPTER XVII

YOU LITTLE FOOL!

AFTER Betsy Gammon drowned, I led the children home.

As we approached the first hamlet, I saw men walking down the main street carrying torches. Some were armed with clubs; one, probably an ex-soldier, had a sword in his belt. No doubt they were a search party.

I didn't want to get too close. My

pointy shoes would identify me as a witch, and they might think I'd been party to the abductions—which, with a twinge of guilt, I acknowledged was true.

"That's my dad and my uncle!" one little boy exclaimed, a smile widening on his face.

"Go to them!" I commanded the other children. "They'll take you home."

Some ran toward the distant figures eagerly, while others walked behind with far less enthusiasm. I put my hand on Emily's shoulder.

"You come with me," I said softly. "I'll take you home myself."

She came with me happily. I took hold of her hand, and we stepped off the path and skirted the hamlet before heading toward the village where Lizzie had seized her.

As we approached her house, I noted that it was in darkness. That wasn't promising. Of course, her mam might have gone to join another search party, or she could be staying with friends or family.

But then it got worse. I saw that the front door was still unlocked.

I eased it open and slowly climbed the stairs, Emily at my heels. Neither of us said anything, but she began to cry softly. We both feared the worst.

When we reached the darkness of the bedroom, I heard someone breathing. The sounds were harsh, suggesting we were listening to a struggle to draw air into lungs that desperately needed it. I reached into my pocket and pulled out the stub of candle I always carried. I muttered a spell out of habit, realizing as I did so that the words were unnecessary. The candle flared into life.

Emily's mother was on all fours, staring toward us. There was nothing in her eyes that told me she recognized her own daughter. She tried to speak, but only gibberish came out.

Then she tried to stand but immediately collapsed onto her hands and knees again. Emily crouched beside her and wrapped her arms around her mother's neck.

"Oh, Mam! Mam!" she cried. "Don't you know me? It's

me, your daughter, Emily. Can't you speak?"

The poor woman only groaned and rolled her eyes. It might well be that she was dying. Some witches believe that a bad blow to the head can make the brain swell up until it becomes too big for the skull and oozes out of the ears and nose. There was certainly a spell to bring this about.

It was also possible that, despite the damage to her brain, the poor woman would live on, unable to speak or recognize her own daughter.

Could I help her? I wondered. Was my magic strong enough to heal her? I was not sure that I could do anything. Dark magic is useful for fighting enemies and forcing obedience upon others. It can kill, maim, and terrify, but its use in healing is uncertain. Some believe that healers use a more gentle, benign magic.

My magic was probably the wrong kind, but I had to try.

"Stand back, Emily," I said softly. "Let me see if I can do anything to help your mam."

The girl did as I asked, and I knelt down beside her mother, placing my right hand on her head. She just stared at me, her eyes wide, looking utterly bewildered.

I willed the woman to get better. With all my strength I pushed that wish toward her. For a few seconds nothing happened. Then I felt intense warmth spreading down my arm and into my hand.

The expression in the woman's eyes changed. She looked up at me angrily and then pushed my hands away. She got to her feet and stared at her daughter. "Emily!" she cried. "I thought I'd never see you again!"

She went to pick up her daughter and started to cry. Soon both of them were weeping; they seemed to have forgotten all about me. I slipped out of the room, went down the stairs, and left the house.

As I headed back toward Pendle, I thought back over what I'd just done. I'd healed Emily's mam. So my magic could do good as well as the other . . . maybe there was hope for me?

I walked as if in a dream.

Walked? I was almost floating, wafting along effort-lessly toward Pendle.

Brambles moved aside at my approach, low branches raised themselves so that I could have headroom, and butterflies fluttered in my wake.

I even walked through the middle of a small village in broad daylight, my pointy shoes clacking on the cobbles. I willed the people not to see me, and I was instantly invisible to them. There was a small market in the square, and I helped myself to a piece of fruit right in front of the stallholder. He didn't notice a thing, and that rosy-cheeked apple proved to be one of the sweetest and juici-est I'd ever munched. Or perhaps it was just the manner in which I'd taken it that made it taste so delicious!

At one point, as I passed south of the great brooding hill, it rained heavily, a torrential downpour that flattened the wheat in the fields and sent rivulets of rainwater rushing down the incline. But none of it touched me. Not one drop fell upon my head, and my shoes were as dry as if there had been a dusty road beneath my feet.

The inside of my head was filled with music. A choir of unseen stars sang in harmony only for me, and I was consumed with a tremendous sense of exultation. I was stronger than all of them. I was free of Lizzie. Free to do as I wished.

I was powerful, strong, and invulnerable.

Nobody could touch me.

Not Lizzie. Not even Grimalkin.

It was dark by the time I reached the village of Roughlee. I climbed up through the trees toward the cottage of Agnes Sowerbutts. I'd been happy here. I would be happy again.

Didn't I deserve some happiness after all I'd been through?

A light was showing at the window to the left of the front door. I had a secret call that I used to let her know I was on my way. It was the cry of a corpse fowl, slightly modulated so that Agnes would know that it was me and not the random call of a night bird.

But I didn't bother to use it this time. I just *willed* Agnes to know that I was here. And it worked. The door to the cottage opened wide, and I could see her standing in the doorway.

I walked right up to her and gave her a big grin.

She didn't smile back.

She slapped me very hard across the face.

"You little fool!" she cried angrily.

CHAPTER XVIII

THE DARK MOON

"**W**HAT is it, Agnes? What have I done wrong? You should be happy!" I said, my eyes filling with tears. It wasn't the pain. The slap had hurt, but much worse was the way Agnes was looking at me.

She took me by the shoulder and dragged me inside the cottage, slamming the door behind us.

"No witch flaunts her power like that, or it will consume her. And so much power, too. I can smell the stink of it evaporating off your skin! Tell me everything!" she demanded. "Something's happened, something momentous. Tell me all of it!"

So I sat on a stool in the kitchen, facing Agnes, and told her everything I could remember: the leather egg, the meeting with Betsy Gammon, the water witches capturing the children to be sacrificed. Then I told her of my decision to flee the house.

"I was scared, but I knew I had to do something. I was so desperate, I decided to go and ask for the help of the local spook. But the thunder and lightning started, and the rain came down, and I needed shelter. I saw a light ahead and thought it was a farm. When I got closer, I saw that it was a strange black barge on the canal; the light came from candles on the deck. The rain should have put them out, but it didn't. . . ."

Next I told her how I'd stepped onto the barge and climbed down too many steps to see the large throne before talking to the mysterious bargeman.

"What was he like?" Agnes demanded. "Tell me all about him."

"Well, he was invisible at first. Said he couldn't be here in person, but that one day, with my help, he might be able to sit on that throne. For a couple of seconds he appeared above it. Hardly older than me, he was, but he had a smiley face and golden hair. However, it was the way he behaved that got to me. He was kind and friendly, and looked at me like he really cared about me. Ain't many people ever looked at me in that way. Told me I had power inside me and didn't need no spook to help those children—I could do it myself!"

"Did he tell you who he was, Alice? Did he give you his name?"

I shook my head. "He said he was one of the unseen princes of this world."

"You foolish girl! It was the Fiend himself, if I'm not mistaken," Agnes cried, shaking her head.

I looked at her in astonishment. "That can't be true! The

Fiend's ugly and old, with a sly look on his face. He has big curved horns, too—everyone knows that."

"No, girl, there's more to him than that. He can make himself large or small and change his shape to whatever he wants. He could become a handsome golden-haired boy in the twinkling of a maiden's eye—as many have found out, to their cost!"

"But why would the Fiend have used me to save those children? He's of the dark, and yet he helped me to thwart the dark. Why would he do that? It doesn't make sense."

"Yes, it does. It makes perfect sense if you just think about it. He recognized your guilt and remorse for what you'd been involved in. He sensed your desperation to put things right. So he gave you what you needed. Child, he must want you very badly."

"What do you mean—*want* me?"

"He wants your soul, child," Agnes told me. "He wants your allegiance. He wants you to stand at his side and fight the light. Some witches are relatively weak. All they can do is charm away a wart or poison an enemy. Others have a power that can be developed throughout their lives. Lizzie's such a one. She works hard at getting stronger. Each year that she lives, her power grows. But there are a few witches, a very few, with extreme innate power; rare ones who are born incredibly strong. And that's what you are, Alice. I've always known. And the Fiend wants you to use your power to help him. That's why I wanted to look after you and bring you up. I wanted to keep you away from witches who'd awaken those dark abilities within you. But Lizzie took you away . . . and now it's come to this!

"Listen to me. You can't use that power for anyone or anything, or it will destroy you. It comes from the very heart of darkness, and if you use it willy-nilly as you've just done, it will seize you for its own and take your soul. Show me your mark!" Agnes commanded.

"What mark?" I asked.

"Don't try to hide things from me, child. Show me the secret mark that tells of your potential."

I began to tremble. I knew what she meant, but I didn't

even want to think about it. In Pendle, every female child with the potential to become a witch had such a mark. It was a sign of what she could become.

"Where is it, child?"

I pulled up my skirt above my knee to reveal the dark stain on the outside of my left thigh. It had been a thin crescent when I last looked.

"Has it grown?" Agnes asked.

"A bit," I admitted. It definitely seemed thicker now.

"Each time you use magic," Agnes told me, "it will grow larger. The use of dark magic has a cumulative effect on the user. Eventually that crescent will become a full dark moon, and then you will belong to the dark entirely. Your soul will be hard. All human compassion will have left you. Do you understand what I am saying?"

"But what can I do, Aunt?" I cried. "What am I supposed to do?"

"Survive, Alice. That's all you can do. That's all any of us can do. But you can't use that power—certainly not in the way you've just done. You must limit its use. Better not to use it at all."

"But Lizzie will want revenge for what I did to her!"

"What *did* you do?" Agnes asked.

So I told her how I'd saved those children, how I'd killed some of the water witches and driven the rest off, how I'd drowned Betsy Gammon.

"What about Lizzie? She wouldn't just let you walk away after that. What did you do to her?" demanded Agnes.

"Paid her back for what she often does to me," I replied. "I summoned a dozen sprogs and set 'em to work on her. Didn't like that one little bit, did she? She'll come after me, for sure. Those water witches, too—they'll want revenge. Without the use of my magic, I'll be helpless. Could be dead and buried before the week is out, Agnes."

Agnes buried her face in her hands. She didn't speak for a long time, but then she looked up at me. "Yes, you are in great danger. There's nothing for it . . . despite my misgivings, you'll have to use just a bit of your power one last time. Only a bit, mind. Just wish confusion on Lizzie and those slimy sisters. Wish them to forget your part in everything. Make them forget that egg ever existed.

"It's a risk, using your magic even once more, but I can see no other way. I'm not strong enough to keep you safe from her, so go back to Lizzie and continue your training for now. It may not be forever. Sometimes things change when you least expect it; one day you might be free of her."

So I did as Agnes advised. I used a bit of my power one more time. Then, the following day, I trudged unhappily back to Lizzie's cottage.

She seemed bewildered, and for days walked around as if in a dream. Then she went back to normal and started making my life difficult again. But it had worked. She never mentioned that leather egg or the water witches. It was as if it had never happened.

My training as a witch continued, but I always hid from Lizzie what I was really capable of. I knew that Agnes was right. It was the Fiend who had spoken to me that night, awakening my latent power. If I kept using it, eventually I would belong to him. My heart would harden, and I would become an evil entity without human feelings. I wouldn't let that happen.

Agnes was proved right in another way, too. My time with Lizzie came to an end just when I least expected it. She led us back to Chipenden, intending to rescue Mother Malkin from the pit in the Spook's garden and then slay him.

But things didn't work out as she hoped.

It was then that I first met Thomas Ward, Old Gregory's apprentice, and my life changed forever. My time as the friend of the Spook's apprentice has been the happiest of my life.

CHAPTER XIX
AN OLD ENEMY

A<small>LL</small> that had happened years earlier, but now, down here in the dark, as I looked at Betsy Gammon, it seemed like only yesterday.

   She smirked at me from her chair, set against the dank cellar wall. The deep, dirty pond was to her right. Water witches were probably waiting beneath the surface.

"Didn't expect to come face-to-face with me again, did you, girl?"

I turned back toward Thorne, my betrayer, ready with angry words, but she had already disappeared. I could hear the sound of her pointy shoes receding up the steps.

"It's sad when people let you down, isn't it?" Betsy said, coming to her feet and taking a step toward me. "But everyone has their price, and Thorne is no exception."

I stared at her, feeling hurt. I'd thought that Thorne was my friend. How could the girl who'd fought alongside Grimalkin have changed so much? The witch assassin had nothing but praise for her.

"Do you know what her price was?" Betsy asked.

I didn't answer. I was considering my options. My best chance was to escape up the steps. But no doubt someone or something would be there now, ready to stop me.

"It's possible for a witch to be born again. Did you know that, girl?"

"Some believe it, but I've never met a witch who claimed to be leading a second life," I replied.

"Oh, it's very rare," Betsy continued. "Takes a lot of power, it does. At least two of the Old Gods have to combine their will to achieve it. And it requires special skill to detect the position of a living person who enters the dark. The best at that is Morwena, the most powerful of the water witches. The moment she knew you'd entered the dark, she got to work. So Thorne was promised another chance to live on earth in return for leading you here. She badly wants an opportunity to prove herself the greatest witch assassin of all—even greater than her teacher, Grimalkin. The chance to become that is to be her reward. Morwena put her in your path and told her to wait. You followed her without a second thought. She led you to us like a lamb!"

Again I made no comment. I had meant to ask Thorne how she'd known where to find me, but I'd never gotten around to it. Now I knew. Agnes was right; I was a fool.

"It's all over for you now, girl. There's nothing you can do to save yourself. You've got powerful magic, but it won't help this time. You see, dark magic doesn't work in the basilica and the area around it. It's a forbidden zone. And there's lots of us and only one of you!"

Betsy put two fingers in her mouth and gave a long, piercing whistle. Immediately, in response, a dozen witches surged out of the water. Some dragged themselves up onto the muddy floor; others soared out like salmon and landed on their webbed and taloned feet, water cascading off them. They glared at me with hungry eyes.

Water witches normally begin by drowning their prey. They drag it into the water, and while it's drowning, they begin to suck its blood—so quickly that the heart stops before drowning can take place.

Alternatively they might just rip me to pieces. Either way, I expected it to be quick.

Perhaps Betsy had lied about not being able to use magic? I thought. I didn't want my life to end here. I had to find the dagger. We had to put an end to the Fiend.

So I exerted my will.

Nothing.

No response.

Magic really *didn't* work here.

I had failed to get the dagger that Tom needed. Now the Fiend would triumph and my best friend would die, too. It had all been for nothing. I was filled with anger.

If this was the end of me, at least I would hurt Betsy one more time.

I kicked out hard, and the point of my shoe went deep into her fat belly. The air came out of her with a *whoosh*, and she doubled over and fell to her knees.

But then many clawed hands seized me and dragged me toward the water. I struggled, but they were extremely strong, and there were too many of them. Fanged teeth appeared inches from my face. Rancid breath filled my nostrils. Then the water closed over my head, and I felt myself being pulled down. It happened so quickly that I hadn't time to take a breath, and as I sank into the murk, water rushed up my nose and into my open mouth. I was choking, drowning, desperate for air.

I thrashed about but couldn't tear myself out of the relentless grip of my enemies. After a while all grew dark, and I felt my consciousness fading away. All I could hear was the *thump-thump* of my heart, slower and slower. Perhaps they were draining my blood. If so, there was no pain other than that in my chest—the frantic need to breathe.

Then there was nothing.

Nothing at all.

The next thing I knew, I was back on the muddy bank on my hands and knees, retching.

"Did you enjoy that, girl?" Betsy gloated, once more seated in her chair. On either side of me, a water witch gripped my shoulder with a taloned hand. "Now you know what it's like to be drowning. You know how I felt when you did that to me. But it's not over yet! Soon as you've got your breath back, it starts all over again. A very slow and painful death is what I plan for you!"

She was as good as her word. Within a minute, I was dragged back into the water again. By now there were only two water witches present, but I would have been helpless against just one.

This time I managed to suck in a deep breath first. But

all that did was delay my agony. Once again the pressure in my lungs was so great that I was forced to breathe out, and soon the water was rushing into my nose and mouth once more.

There was a roaring in my ears; darkness. Then, once again, I found myself on my knees, gasping for air and vomiting water.

I lost count of how many times the process was repeated. On each occasion Betsy taunted and gloated from her chair while I went through the agonizing process of recovery.

But everything must come to an end.

I looked up for the umpteenth time, water pouring from my nose and mouth, trying to draw in a first painful breath, when I realized that it was Betsy who had come to an end.

She was sitting back, slumped in her chair, a knife buried up to its hilt in her throat. Even as I watched, I saw her body start to disintegrate. Her head had fallen off now, and was sliding down between her knees. I vaguely remember wondering if that was what usually happened when you died for the second time.

Moments later, I knew the answer.

There were no taloned hands gripping my shoulders any longer. The two water witches were lying beside me, stretched out on the muddy floor of the cellar. Each had a knife between her shoulder blades. Their bodies were starting to crumble, too.

A hand seized my arm and yanked me to my feet. I came face-to-face with Thorne and angrily tried to pull away. But I was too weak, still fighting for breath.

"Come on! Come on!" she screamed into my face. "Morwena could arrive at any moment."

She dragged me toward the steps and pulled me up to the top. I was too feeble to resist.

We crossed the room and went out through the front door. I staggered across the marshy ground with Thorne. Finally we crouched in the shadow of a stone wall, out of the light of the blood moon.

"I'm sorry." Thorne's voice was hardly more than a whisper.

I was about to give her a piece of my mind, but my

stomach lurched, everything began to spin, and I leaned sideways and vomited into the grass.

At last I got my breath back and blasted her with my anger.

"You're sorry? *Sorry?* Sorry for what? For betraying me and sending me to my death? Sorry for stopping me from getting the dagger and destroying the Fiend? And who would he go after first? Ain't much doubt about it! Grimalkin, I think, because of what she's done. Fine way to repay someone who trained you! Grimalkin wouldn't be pleased with what you did. You were brave in life; she hoped you'd be brave in death. That's what she told me. But you weren't brave, were you? You were a coward who couldn't face being in the dark and would do *anything* for the chance at a second life!"

Thorne said nothing. She just bowed her head and stared down at the ground.

After a while my anger began to ebb away, and I spoke again. "Why did you come back?"

She replied without looking up. "Even before I reached

the top of the steps, I regretted what I'd done. It hadn't seemed real until then. Then I heard what was happening below. You drowned Betsy back on earth, but her death was nothing compared to what you would experience. I couldn't bear it. So I came down to help you."

"What now?" I asked.

"I'll help you to get the dagger."

"I would be better off on my own," I retorted. "How can I trust you after that? Did you talk to anybody else when you left the cellar? Did you tell 'em why I'm here—that I have to reach the Fiend's domain?"

That was important. If they knew what I wanted and where I was going, they'd be there waiting for me.

"No, Alice, I didn't have time. They still don't know. . . . So think about it. You've more chance with me than on your own; we need each other. After what I just did, they'll be after me too. No doubt they'll plan a horrible, slow second death for me. You're close now to where you want to go. The domains move around, but they say the Fiend's domain is always near this one with its basilica for worship. There's a good chance that this gate will take us there. Trust me again, please. Let me help you."

I thought carefully. There was truth in what she'd just said. And she *had* come back for me.

"I need to get into the basilica and avoid the trap they've set," I told Thorne. "I must reach that gate. Can you help me to do that?"

"Inside the basilica, we'll have to trust to luck. I've never been in there myself, and the gate could be anywhere— we'll have to search for it. But I might be able to get us inside unobserved. I know those who might help. But you'll have to wait here. It'll be easier and faster if I go alone."

"How long will you be?"

"As long as it takes. Just wait."

Then Thorne was gone, and I was alone in the shadow of the wall, shivering in my wet clothes.

CHAPTER XX
JAWS WIDE OPEN

IT was hard to judge the passing of
time, and I crouched there, wet and
uncomfortable, for what seemed like
an hour or more.

I began to wonder if Thorne would
ever return. Maybe she'd changed her
mind again and sided with my enemies
once more. Perhaps she'd been caught.

I could wait only a little while longer.

There was no way of knowing how much time had passed back on earth—it could already be close to Halloween. Soon I would have to try and find my own way into the basilica.

But finally Thorne reappeared and, without a word of explanation, crooked her finger in a sign that I should follow her.

Keeping mostly to back alleys, we approached the basilica in a slow widdershins spiral. We arrived at the side of the huge building. Between us and the wall was a large paved area, perhaps a hundred paces across. Whether we faced south, north, east, or west, it was impossible to say in a domain where the blood moon remained fixed in the same position.

Thorne came to a halt, and as we dropped into a crouch, she pointed. "Do you see the third door from the left?" she asked.

I counted quickly. There were five doors of varying sizes. The third, oval in shape, was the smallest of them all. I nodded.

"That's the best way in. I've been told it isn't usually guarded," Thorne told me.

"Do you trust the people you spoke to?" I said.

"As much as you can trust anybody who's been in the dark for some time. The longer you're here, the more desperate you become. I spoke to a group of people and trust some more than others. But all agreed that was the door to use."

I wasn't filled with confidence, but I had to take the risk. I nodded again, and Thorne pointed toward the door and put her finger to her lips before setting off immediately. I followed at her heels.

We were less than fifty strides from the door we'd been directed to when I heard a bell begin to toll—the one that summoned the chosen to be slain in the basilica, and then the random taking of blood. Now we were in immediate danger.

At the thirteenth toll of that dreadful bell, something shrieked out from above. I recognized it immediately—the raucous cry of a chyke. And it wasn't alone. Others were swooping down toward us, a dozen or more of the batlike creatures, their clawed hands extended to rend our flesh, their eyes glowing red like embers. Last time I had estimated the creature to be of approximately human size, but these appeared even larger.

Thorne had her blades, but I had no weapons at all, and as I'd just learned, to my cost, magic didn't work near the basilica. I decided to try again anyway. I flicked at the nearest chyke with my mind—a spell of repulsion. It didn't work. The creature continued to glide toward me, its open jaws dripping saliva.

We began to run toward the shelter of the dark oval doorway.

The chyke attacked, swooping down, and I dived forward into a roll. But not before I felt a sharp pain in my forehead. When I scrambled to my feet, blood was running into my eyes, but Thorne had returned to stand over me and, despite the pain she must be feeling in her hands, was holding two blades and trying to drive away the attacker.

I glanced about me and knew a moment of real terror.

Other chykes were coming for us, too many for Thorne to fend off alone. We were about to be ripped to pieces.

I lurched to my feet, holding my arms high to protect my face. I anticipated the tearing of my flesh, but there was no pain. Instead, the claws that had been aiming for my face were gone. I looked up and saw the chykes fleeing from another, larger winged being. One was too late and, screaming in terror, was seized by its pursuer. It was quickly ripped asunder, the bloody pieces falling onto the flags behind us.

My stomach turned over as I saw the killer banking and flying toward us. The rest of the chykes had fled. Were we its new prey? I wondered. But then I recognized the predator.

"It's Wynde, the lamia who died before the walls of Malkin Tower," Thorne said. "She was a friend in life and will be so in death."

Grimalkin had told me that she had watched from the battlements of the tower, unable to help, as Wynde had been slain by the kretch. It had eaten her heart, thus sending her directly to the dark. But the lamia witch had fought bravely, and others had to help the kretch to overcome her, among them the dark mage Bowker and three witches who had speared Wynde with knives on long poles.

Later Grimalkin had slain them all.

Wynde landed close to us. "Why have you, who still live and breathe, entered the dark?" she demanded of me. "Why have you risked so much?"

Her voice was guttural and her words difficult to make out. Sometimes when a lamia was in the process of shape-shifting toward the feral, she temporarily lost the use of language altogether. In this final winged form it usually returned, but it was still difficult to understand what she was saying.

"I am here to gain the means to destroy the Fiend. The gate I need to reach his domain is somewhere inside the basilica, and I must use it," I told her. "There is something vital there that I must retrieve."

"Enemies wait for you beyond that door," she rasped.

Thorne scowled. "You've been betrayed again, Alice, but

it wasn't of my doing, I swear it. The friends I spoke of were witches who sometimes cared for me after my cruel father beat me. I hoped they could be trusted. I'm sorry. I've let you down again."

"You did your best, Thorne," I told her.

"There is another entrance, a high one in the roof," said Wynde. "I will carry you up to it. Who will be first?"

"Go first!" Thorne commanded. "You've no weapons."

There was no time to argue. Wynde flapped her wings and hovered before me, her scaly knees level with my face.

"Grab on to my legs!" she commanded.

I'd barely managed to get a proper hold before she lurched upward; the ground receded at a terrifying speed. Moments later she was flying toward the dark mass of the basilica. I was facing backward, and the first indication I had that we were over it was when we passed the tower, the tip of the lamia's wing almost brushing the stones. Then she folded her wings close to her body and plummeted down like a stone. I gasped as I left my stomach behind.

The roof rushed up to meet us, but at the last moment

Wynde unfurled her wings, and my feet made contact with the tiles. I released my grip on her legs, and she flew up again, returning to collect Thorne.

I looked around. I was standing with my back to a huge buttress that supported the square tower. Ahead of me was a narrow path leading between two sloping roofs to a wall with a narrow door in it. Was that a way into the basilica? We couldn't now be seen by those on the ground, but some would have noted our journey with the lamia. Now others within the building might be racing to intercept us. We needed to move quickly.

I waited impatiently for the lamia to bring Thorne to me. What was taking so long? I had a moment of fear. What if in the meantime she'd been attacked by the chykes again? How long could she hope to hold such a fierce flock at bay?

Then I heard the beating of wings and sighed with relief as Wynde lowered Thorne to stand beside me. Hovering before us, the winged lamia pointed at the door with a taloned hand.

"That is the way," she confirmed. "There may be others

inside who are willing to help, but whether they can fight their way to you is uncertain."

"We thank you for your help," I told her.

"Thank me by getting what you seek. Thank me by putting an end to the Fiend!" she cried. Then she soared aloft, flew round the tower, and was lost to sight.

Wasting no time, we hurried toward the door. There was no visible handle. What if it was locked? I asked myself. The spell of opening wouldn't work in this place.

But I needn't have feared. It opened at the pressure of my hand and swung inward, its hinges groaning. It was very dark inside, and I reached for the candle in my pocket. But as I brought it out, I remembered that without magic I wouldn't be able to light it. Thorne shrugged, then squeezed past me and went through the door slowly, her hands extended before her. She was touching the wall, feeling her way in the dark.

"It seems to be a spiral staircase," she said, her voice hardly more than a whisper. "It goes counterclockwise. Feel for the rail on the right."

Pushing the candle back into my pocket, I went through the open doorway cautiously. Sliding my hand down the rail, I steadied myself as I descended the stone steps, following the spiral downward. Hemmed in by cold stone walls on both sides, I felt claustrophobic. There was no way to stop our pointy shoes from clacking on the stone steps, and I hoped that nothing was waiting for us below. It would have plenty of warning of our arrival.

We must have gone down at least a couple of hundred steps when I noticed a yellow flickering light from below, which allowed me to see Thorne's silhouette. The constant turning left was starting to make me feel dizzy, and it seemed to be getting warmer, which wasn't helping.

We emerged onto a narrow ledge, and glancing beyond it, my dizziness grew worse and I almost fell forward. The space I gazed upon was vast and the ground lay far below. It resembled some gigantic cavern, and my first thought was that the inside of the basilica was somehow larger than the outside. Then I remembered the house where Betsy Gammon had been the keeper of the water witches, and realized that the effect was due to something similar. The lowest level of the basilica had been excavated in the same way. Its floor was far lower than the ground outside the building.

Nothing seemed to be moving below, but I could see a number of structures. Were they altars to the various Old Gods of the dark?

"Where's the gate, then?" I said, immediately realizing I had made a mistake. I had kept my voice low, but it was amplified by the vast inner area of the basilica and echoed from wall to wall.

Had I further alerted our enemies to our presence?

In response to my question, Thorne put a warning finger against her lips and pointed downward.

But how could we get there? The narrow ledge didn't slope down. It ran along the wall at the same height. However, Thorne set off along the ledge, taking slow, careful steps. I kept my eyes on her right shoulder, the one nearest the wall, not daring to glance into the scary abyss. Beyond her I saw an archway in the wall. When Thorne ducked her head and stepped inside it, I followed. Narrow steps led into the dark, slowly becoming wider, the dank walls pressing in on either side.

Once again the thought came to me that someone or something would be waiting for us below. Could it be that our every move was known? Again I had the sense of being watched. This time it was stronger than ever.

I could see flickering lights ahead. Below us lay a chamber, with candles in wall brackets.

Thorne whispered, "We're getting closer to the gate. But if it *is* there, then so are our enemies. They control it."

She was still going down, but her steps were slowing. Then she suddenly stopped completely. "Go back!" she shouted, spinning round to face me and gesticulating wildly. "It's a trap! I can see enemies waiting below!"

But it was already too late. Heavy boots thudded down the steps behind us. I couldn't see who they were, but I knew that there were too many boots and too many enemies. We were trapped.

Thorne drew her blades and then ran the steps toward

the chamber. I followed hard on her heels. Once on level ground, I stood at her right shoulder and stared at the occupants of the small, windowless room we found ourselves in.

There were three of them.

Two were dressed in the garb of Pendle witches, with tattered black gowns and pointy shoes. The third was a huge abhuman with too many teeth to fit into his mouth.

I faced three old enemies: Bony Lizzie, Mother Malkin, and Tusk.

CHAPTER XXI
A NEW THREAT

I should have realized that at least one of the enemies I had bested on earth would be waiting in the basilica to get their revenge.

Tusk, the abhuman, had been slain by Old Gregory, the Chipenden spook. Soon after that, Tom Ward had used salt and iron to weaken Mother Malkin, and in her desperation to escape she had fled across the pigpen at the Ward family farm. Those hungry pigs had eaten every bit of her, including her heart, sending her into the dark forever.

She was small—Tom Ward's use of salt and iron had shrunk her to a third of her previous size. And now, after death, she was trapped in that form, but she was still terribly dangerous.

Bony Lizzie had been bound in a pit by John Gregory until war had come to the County and the Pendle witches had rescued her. My final confrontation with her had been on the Isle of Mona. Tom and I had pursued her, and she had fallen off a cliff into the sea. Destroyed by saltwater, her heart eventually eaten by fish, she too was trapped in the dark and would be desperate for revenge.

"Well, daughter," Lizzie said, a gloating smile on her face. "At last I have the chance to pay you back. Now we will make *you* suffer!"

Old Mother Malkin shuffled forward, too. I saw that her long white hair was matted with dirt. Magic didn't work here, but once this gnarled old witch had been the most powerful in the County, and her wrinkled body would still show a terrible, inhuman strength. Although she barely came up to my knees, her talons were extended toward me, her glowing red eyes desperate for my blood.

I took a step backward; Thorne took a step forward.

"Well, look what the cat's dragged in!" Lizzie exclaimed. "Morwena ain't going to like the way you've gone back on your word. She won't be best pleased—she'll be cutting more than your thumbs away!"

Thorne didn't waste words on replying. She never even looked at Lizzie. A blade was in her hand, and she slashed horizontally at Mother Malkin, opening a wide red mouth in her wrinkled forehead.

The old witch screamed and staggered back, blood cascading down into her eyes and blinding her. I attacked, too, and struck at Lizzie with my left hand, my nails narrowly missing her eyes.

But before I could do anything more, I was seized by Tusk. He grabbed me from behind, pinned my arms to my sides, and lifted me up so that my feet were clear of the ground. I kicked back at his knees with the heels of my pointy shoes, but he began to squeeze me so that I could hardly breathe.

Tighter and tighter he clasped me, until I felt as if my ribs would snap. I could no longer draw air into my lungs. He was killing me. My only hope was that Thorne would somehow intervene and cut him down.

"Let her go! Let her go!" cried Thorne.

"Then drop your blades!" Lizzie screeched back at her.

By then my vision had grown dark, but I heard the sound of her blades clanking on the ground. There were other noises, too—more heavy boots running down the steps and coming into the room behind us.

We were finished. Now I would never be able to get the dagger. The chance to destroy the Fiend would be lost.

The next thing I knew, I was lying facedown on a cold stone floor. A woman's voice spoke somewhere behind me.

"She's awake. Now I'll teach her all about suffering!"

There was a sudden sharp pain in my ribs. I knew it was

a jab from a pointy shoe, and I recognized the voice. I had been kicked by Bony Lizzie—my own mother.

I rolled into a ball, attempting to protect myself, but was dragged to my feet by a fist bunched in my hair. Lizzie's eyes were glaring into mine. She looked insane with rage.

"Now you'll get your comeuppance, girl!" she shrieked, showering me with spittle. Almost ripping my hair out by the roots, she twisted me away from her so that I fell back into Tusk's arms once more. He roared at me, opening his mouth wide. The foul breath was a hot wind in my face, making me retch. The yellow tusks were almost touching my cheeks, and there were a lot more sharp teeth inside his mouth—two double rows of them.

For a moment I thought he was going to bite off my nose or tear a chunk of flesh from my face, but instead he gave me an evil grin, set me down on my feet, and turned me round to face a dark doorway opposite the steps. When I turned back to face the witches, I saw that Lizzie had a blade in each hand, pointing toward me.

These were the blades that Thorne had been holding.

The assassin was being held by a couple of the brutish men who had followed us down the stairs. Others were standing behind her—perhaps a dozen in all. I thought I recognized a couple of them as yeomen who had served Lizzie on the Isle of Mona, where she had attempted to become queen.

For a second I gazed into Thorne's eyes. Even though she didn't speak, somehow I understood that not all was lost. She had dropped her blades and surrendered in order to save me. Otherwise I would have died, my ribs caved in and the life squeezed from my body by Tusk. They had disarmed her; I could see no other blades in the scabbards set in the leather straps crisscrossing her chest.

However, I knew that Thorne's armory was a duplication of Grimalkin's. There was a smaller sheath just under her left arm containing another weapon—the scissors that were used to snip off the thumb bones of a slain witch.

But for my desperate plight at the hands of Tusk, Thorne would still have been fighting. And I knew that at the first favorable opportunity, she would fight again.

Thorne had said that the gate could be somewhere in this

room. I glanced about me quickly but could see nothing. What would it look like, anyway? Gates took on different shapes and could be manipulated by those who controlled them.

"That way!" Lizzie snapped, pushing me toward the doorway.

I stepped forward to enter another room. This one was long and narrow—no more than three people could walk abreast. On the floor lay a bloodred carpet. I walked directly ahead of Lizzie, Tusk, and Mother Malkin, trying not to show my fear.

I was prodded along, blade points pricking my back, toward the shadowed recess at the far end. As we approached it, my first thought was that it contained a throne, but then I saw a hooded figure slouched on a simple wooden chair with a high back. Dressed in a gown and hood, he could easily have been mistaken for a spook. Set on each side of him was a big bucket. And I didn't have to look to know what the buckets contained. The stink told me.

It was an unmistakable metallic, coppery smell.

The two buckets were filled with blood.

I glanced about me, aware that all eyes were locked upon the rich blood in the bucket—the currency in the dark. But my attention was quickly drawn back to the hooded figure.

Slowly the head lifted, and I saw golden eyes gleaming at me from within the darkness of the hood. They were vast, at least five or six times bigger than those usually found in a human face.

What exactly *was* the creature facing me? Another abhuman like Tusk? I wondered.

Very slowly the entity raised its left hand toward its face. The fingers were long and bony and seemed to be covered in short black bristles. They drew back the hood to reveal what had been hidden within its shadows.

But the face! The horror of that terrible face! The eyes were multifaceted, bulbous, and huge. And each one contained the image of a terrified girl. It took me a couple of moments to realize that I was gazing at my own reflection over and over again.

The head was that of a giant fly, covered in dark hair,

with a long, flickering tongue. It was a being straight out of my worst nightmares.

I remembered again that day when we had set out to kill the old spook Jacob Stone. Lizzie had bitten the heads off thirteen rats and attracted a swarm of large black flies in order to gather sufficient magic to be able to move two large stones and free the dead witches. Lizzie had told me that the source of her power had been the dark lieutenant who sat at the left-hand side of the Fiend. And now, after death, she had clearly become his disciple and servant in the dark.

I was facing the demon Beelzebub, sometimes called the Lord of the Flies.

"Well, girl," Lizzie snapped from behind me. "You always feared flies. But nothing you ever saw on earth will match this. You're going to get exactly what you deserve! Now I remember how you cheated me of the power inside that leather egg. Well, it's time to pay you back for everything!"

The tongue of the demon rasped in and out of the mouth, making a strange grating, vibrating sound. Was Beelzebub attempting to speak to me?

A moment later I realized that it was indeed some kind of communication—but it was not directed at me.

It was a command.

The Lord of the Flies had summoned his own special creatures to his presence.

It began as a faint buzzing, which steadily increased in volume. Suddenly a fly was circling my head—a bluebottle as big as a bumblebee. It was quickly joined by a couple more, and then another. And it was only when the number increased to a dozen or more that I saw where the flies were coming from.

They were erupting from Beelzebub's open mouth, a steady line of them flying out faster and faster to swarm about my head. I cried out in fear, remembering how, back in Jacob Stone's garden, they had settled on Lizzie's face, obscuring every inch of it, even landing on her tongue. I was filled with a claustrophobic terror at the thought of that happening to me. But the flies quickly left me and descended in two clouds onto the buckets of blood on either side of the demon.

They were still hurtling out of that hideous mouth, darting past the long, rasping tongue to form a living, writhing mound of flies, a dark, pulsating lid on each bucket of blood.

Moments later the two swarms left the buckets and joined into one huge cloud less than two feet from my face. Their drone became a roar, and I tried to step back, immediately feeling the sharp points of two blades against my back as I did so.

The dark cloud began to contract into a rough oval. Then, out of that simple egg shape, a more complex structure began to form. At first I thought it was just my imagination. I often see images like that in clouds, or even in the leaves of shrubs and trees. If you look hard enough, faces are everywhere.

But I knew that my imagination was playing no part here. The swarm had taken on the shape of a huge face with a hooked nose, bulbous eyes, and a wide-open mouth that showed two sets of sharp teeth. And there was a further touch of horror.

The flies had been feeding on the blood from the buckets.

Some of them must have been immersed in it, under the weight of those pressing down from above. Now those flies had formed the lips and teeth of the huge face, and they were covered in blood.

Suddenly I detected a faint smell of rotting eggs. *The gate must be somewhere nearby,* I realized. I looked about me, searching for a glint of maroon, but could see nothing.

The mouth moved and the buzzing changed, became deeper.

It was speaking to me.

"You are the daughter of my master!" cried the humming, rasping voice. "Why have you betrayed him? You could have had so much. Why have you turned against him? Power was yours, simply for the asking!"

I shook my head. "Ain't nothing I wanted from him," I said. "Better not to have been born than have him for a father and that dirty witch behind me for a mam."

That earned me a kick from Lizzie, but I bit my lip to stop myself crying out from the pain. Didn't want to give her the satisfaction, did I?

"Why are you here?" asked that huge mouth. "Why have you entered the dark?"

It seemed to me that, maimed as he was, the Fiend might somehow have discovered my intent and passed it on to his servants. But perhaps Tom's mam had been able to cloak her plan from him *and* from his servants in the dark. They didn't know that we hoped to destroy him by means of the ritual. Tom's mam had hobbled him once, and he'd snatched the blade and taken it into the dark. But if they didn't already know that I was here to get that dagger—the third hero sword, the Dolorous Blade—it might not take them long to work it out. I certainly wasn't going to give anything away.

Didn't want 'em waiting for me in the Fiend's throne room, did I, when I went to get it?

There was still hope. Thorne had her scissors—but would she get the chance to use them? Or would they kill us both right here and now?

I was waiting for my chance, too. I couldn't use magic here, but I had no intention of giving up without a fight.

CHAPTER XXII
The Bones of Beelzebub

"**D**ON'T keep him waiting for an answer!" Lizzie screeched into my ear. "You wouldn't believe what he's capable of!"

"I will give you one more opportunity to answer," said the mouth, opening and closing, dripping blood as the flies droned each word. "I know your secret fear. Remain silent and it will happen to you now!"

My secret fear! What did Beelzebub mean? I had many fears: that I might not manage to retrieve the dagger; that I would return too late for the ritual to be performed; that something might have happened to Tom; that Grimalkin would fail to keep the head safe and that the Fiend would walk the earth again; that I would lack the courage to keep silent when Tom took my bones; that one day I would be struck by lightning; that—

Suddenly I knew what the demon meant. A memory flashed into my mind to make me shudder. Once more I saw Lizzie in Jacob Stone's garden, flies crawling all over her face.

That was what I feared here and now, and Beelzebub knew it! Creepy-crawlies. After spiders, I feared swarms of flies. I couldn't bear the thought of them crawling over my face.

"Tell him nothing!" Thorne cried out.

I glanced across to where she was still held by two brutish thugs. I nodded. She was right. I couldn't tell them why I had entered the dark.

"So be it!" said the mouth, which immediately closed. The features melted back into the simple oval that had given birth to them. Then the swarm of flies soared aloft and zoomed toward me.

I lashed out with my hands, trying to keep them away. But it was hopeless. There was more chance of fending off hailstones with a sewing needle. In seconds, the flies were all over my face and head. They covered my eyes so that I couldn't see, buzzed into my ears and up my nose. I felt the weight of them bowing my head forward.

My nose was blocked and I couldn't breathe . . . I panicked. There was only one thing I could do—something I was desperate to avoid.

I needed to open my mouth to draw in a lungful of precious air. . . .

But if I did that, the flies would be able to get in.

I reached for my nose and squashed as many as I could, feeling them turn to slime under my desperate fingers. I squeezed my nostrils together and sneezed out the flies.

But I had less than a second's relief before they crawled up my nose again. Strong hands seized mine and pulled my fingers away from my face so that I could not gain even a moment's further relief.

I hung on as long as I could, my lungs bursting, enduring the horror of those big, fat bluebottles crawling all over my face and getting tangled in my hair.

Then at last I had no choice.

I opened my mouth and gulped in air.

And the flies followed.

I tried spitting them out, but there were far too many of them. They were all over my tongue, and I began to retch as they crawled down my throat. Moments later, that too was blocked. I fell to my knees, gagging because of the flies in my throat, and then vomited. That gave me another second of relief, one brief fresh intake of air before they filled my mouth and throat once more.

My wrists were still held tightly, my arms now twisted behind my back. My eyes were covered and I couldn't breathe; I was in darkness, slowly dying.

Suddenly the weight was gone from my head, and I saw the flickering yellow of torchlight. The swarm had lifted off me and was shifting to form a gigantic face again. I spat the last of the flies out of my mouth and looked up at it.

Out of the corner of my eye I could see Tusk, still behind me. He was holding my wrists so tightly that the bones were being crushed. Lizzie was now on my right, a gloating smile on her face.

"Never did like flies, did you, girl?" she said. "They seem to like *you*, though—can't get enough of you!"

The huge mouth opened again, and words rumbled out. "Speak now. Tell me what I want!"

I shook my head and stared up at the swarm defiantly.

"You are brave and can endure difficult trials," said the gigantic mouth. "But I sense another weakness within you. Another fear. You would not let harm befall a friend whom you have the power to save. Bring the other girl closer!"

Lizzie stepped aside to allow the two men to drag Thorne forward to my side.

"This time I will not relent until you tell me what I wish to know," said the voice. "And if you refuse, she who is your friend will die the second death!"

The face became a dark egg again and moved up closer to the ceiling, forming an angry swarm, ready to descend upon Thorne.

I was beaten. I would have to tell the demon what he wanted.

We were prisoners, and our hopes of ever achieving our goal were slim. What little hope I had now rested on Thorne finding an opportunity to set us free by using her remaining weapon—the scissors.

She couldn't do that if I allowed the flies to smother her. So what would it matter then if they knew I'd come here for the dagger?

I opened my mouth, intending to tell Beelzebub what he wished to know. . . .

But in that second, Thorne tore herself free. It happened very quickly. She drew the scissors from their sheath, but instead of using these on her captors, she ran straight toward the chair where Beelzebub was seated.

He was a demon, but he had only been able to manipulate the flies because they were part of him, part of who he was; they were like extra limbs, particles of self that he could direct using his mind. Anywhere else but within this basilica, and he would have blasted Thorne with powerful magic, hurling her across the room or incinerating her on the spot. But even his demonic magic didn't work here.

Thorne was fast. She took Beelzebub by surprise. At the last moment, his tongue flickering in and out of his mouth, he came to his feet and tried to fend off her attack with his left hand.

That was a mistake. Probably the biggest he'd ever made in the countless eons he'd spent in the dark.

He had never met a human as brave and fast and deadly as Thorne. She had been trained by Grimalkin. She thought like Grimalkin. She fought like Grimalkin.

And, like Grimalkin, Thorne dared things that some couldn't even imagine!

The scissors flashed as they caught the light from the

nearest of the torches. The blades closed.

And she snipped the thumb from the demon's left hand.

Beelzebub screamed and brought up his right hand to protect himself.

She took that thumb, too.

She caught each thumb as it fell, holding them in her left hand as the demon staggered backward, shrieking like a stuck pig.

At that moment I once more became aware of that faint stink of rotting eggs. Was it the gate? I sniffed quickly three times, and to my astonishment, my eyes were drawn toward the swarm of flies. They were losing the egg shape, beginning to form something else.

Then Thorne whirled to meet a new threat. It was Tusk, roaring like a bull and lumbering toward her, ready to rip her limb from limb while Lizzie and Mother Malkin stood immobile, mouths open, paralyzed with shock.

She was ready for him. I knew exactly what she would do before she struck. I remembered how John Gregory had dealt with Tusk back in the County. He had stabbed him through the forehead with the silver-alloy blade of his spook's staff. Pierced to the brain, Tusk had fallen down stone-dead.

Now Thorne did the same, but with her scissors. Quickly she stepped within Tusk's lumbering grasp. As his arms closed to try and crush her, she struck. For a moment the scissors were left sticking out of the center of Tusk's forehead. He made no sound, but his grasping hands sank to his side and he fell to his knees, eyes already glassy.

She plucked the scissors free, looked directly at me, and then pointed to the swarm of flies. "The gate!" she shouted.

The swarm was no longer in the shape of an egg; neither had it formed the face that had allowed Beelzebub to speak to us. They had become three large concentric circles, their color changing from black to maroon, and they were flying rapidly widdershins, making it look as if those hoops were spinning. Within those circles was something else.

Another domain.

I could see columns and dark arches . . . some sort of building.

"Go through it, Alice! You first!" cried Thorne.

For a moment I hesitated. What if I got through and she was left behind?

But I had to find the blade. Everything depended on that. I looked up and saw both Mother Malkin and Lizzie reaching for me with their long, sharp nails.

I ran past them and leaped through the gate of flies.

CHAPTER XXIII
THE BLOOD-FILLED EYE

WE were sitting on wooden stools before a cauldron, and Thorne was holding the demon's thumbs above the boiling water. She wanted the power that wearing them could bring. It would increase our chances of success and survival.

Thorne had followed me through the gate, and at last, just as she had predicted, we found ourselves in the domain of the Fiend. I remembered it from my last visit. There was no doubt. For one thing, there was the pervasive smell—an odor of sulfur, a hint of something being burned. The light was distinctive; it had a strange coppery sheen, as if we were viewing everything through ancient colored glass.

The only difference was that this time his servants, the lesser demons who had tormented and tortured me, were absent. In fact, at present the domain appeared to be deserted.

We were in the large stone-flagged kitchen of some vast building that could have been a castle or a place of worship like the one we'd just left. I had never seen it from the outside, though I had previously spent time in its dungeons and had been dragged in manacles through its interminable dank stone corridors. It was all flooding back to me now, the horror of my earlier visit here.

Cauldrons, pots, pans, and cooking utensils were everywhere. But there were no chefs, and we saw no food. When Thorne dropped the demon's thumbs into the boiling water, they began to cook.

Then I noticed Thorne's own thumbs . . . she had them back. It was as if she had never been mutilated.

"How did that happen?" I asked in astonishment. "Surely it must be the result of magic—but I thought that wasn't possible within the basilica."

She shrugged and smiled. "Maybe it's the result of some natural law of the dark. I came here minus thumbs because having them cut off was what killed me. But here in the dark, I just took the thumbs of Beelzebub, a powerful demon. So I get them back."

"Grimalkin would be proud of you!" I said. "Taking the thumbs of a demon is something that she probably never did."

"She helped take the head of the Fiend, though," said Thorne with a smile.

"How was it that the flies became the gate?" I wondered, watching the thumbs spinning in the boiling water. "I could smell the gate when we faced Beelzebub, but I never guessed it was the flies. I thought they were part of him."

"They were, but I think he had seized the gate to lure us

into his presence. To control it, he had to make it temporarily part of himself. But when I cut off his thumbs, the pain made him lose concentration, and the gate broke free and formed its natural shape, using the flies as a frame."

"Did you know that would happen?"

"I wasn't certain," Thorne replied, "but I thought there was a chance. In any case, I just did what Grimalkin taught me—when you face many enemies, hurt the strongest first."

After a while, the bristly flesh slipped off the white thumb bones, and they danced in the churning water. Thorne got to her feet and leaned over the cauldron, her face intent on what had to be done.

She must pluck the bones out of the scalding water, ignoring the pain. They must be grasped at exactly the same time. Dropping one would cause the magic to be lost.

Thorne moved quickly, her hands a blur, then looked at me, smiling in triumph, one of the demon's thumb bones in each hand.

It took her another half hour to bore a tiny hole in each bone with a blade adapted for the purpose; it was long, thin, and very hard at the tip.

I was impatient to search for the throne room—Tom's mam had told him that the blade was hidden under the Fiend's throne. However, I bit my lip. We needed all the help we could get, and those demon bones would strengthen Thorne considerably.

Once she had finished, she transferred the bones to her necklace to join the others.

"Should be more power in there than in the bones of even the strongest witch," I remarked.

"Then let's hope we don't need it. It's too quiet here, but that won't last."

"Why didn't they just jump through the gate after us?" I asked.

"It was already closing as I leaped through," Thorne replied. "Beelzebub was in too much pain to control it, and it had pulled away from him. But they'll find it again eventually, and then they'll follow us."

"Will they know it leads to the Fiend's domain?"

"That's what they'll guess—although gates don't *always* lead to the same domain. If it moves before they can find it, they won't know where we've gone and will need incredibly strong magic to locate us again. They'll have to be well clear of the basilica to use it. Do *you* know where the Fiend's throne room is?"

I shook my head. "I saw lots of dungeons, but never the throne room. . . . At least, I don't recollect being there. The truth is, it was so terrible that my mind won't let me remember most of it."

"So that's two things we have to search for—the blade, and the gate to get us out of here. Let's look for the blade first," Thorne said.

But the difficulty that faced us soon became apparent. We left the kitchen, went down three flights of stairs to a courtyard, and were faced with a choice of three passageways. We chose the central and widest one, which had a high arched roof.

We hurried along, but after about an hour we had still

not reached its end, nor did we have any idea where it was leading.

"This place is vast," Thorne observed. "We could search for years and still not find it."

It was true. The sheer size of the Fiend's domain made our task nearly impossible.

But we had to plow on. When, after another half hour, we finally reached the end of the passageway, I didn't like what I saw. We found ourselves in a vast, open circular space. Above us was a dome, so high that we might have been looking up at clouds. Before us was a dark gray lake, its waters still and forbidding. Its surface was like glass, and it looked deep enough to hide anything. It filled almost the whole area but for a narrow path that led away to our left, hugging the curved stone wall

Suddenly there was cry from far above—the screech of a corpse fowl. We both looked up and saw the bird flapping across the calm lake toward us. It glided for a few seconds, swooped lower, then curved away, heading back toward the center.

"That's probably Morwena's familiar," I said. "This lake would be the ideal place for her to lurk."

"But we heard that cry back in the last domain," Thorne protested. "How can she be here? The gate closed after me, and they can't have found a way through already."

"We heard her as we first entered the city," I said. "She had plenty of time to use the gate before we faced Beelzebub. And she didn't appear when you killed Betsy and the water witches. So she'd probably already gone then."

"But how would she know we were coming to this domain?"

"She's powerful and crafty. She might have worked it out for herself. As a loyal daughter of the Fiend, she might have been given more information than the rest of his followers. Perhaps she knows about the dagger that Tom's mam used against him before. Don't forget, she was the one who first knew when I entered the dark."

"Even if Morwena is here, together we're a match for her!" asserted Thorne confidently, and I knew she was feeling guilty about being lured by Morwena and Betsy to trick me. "She can only use her bloodeye on one person at a time. Grimalkin told me how she and Tom fought the water witches. They came face-to-face with Morwena, and she paralyzed Grimalkin with her blood-filled eye. But Tom wasn't affected, so he used his silver chain to bind her, bringing her to her knees. That freed Grimalkin, and she killed the water witch. We can do the same. When she puts one of us in thrall, the other can kill her. That way she'll be dead forever—it'll be the end of her."

Thorne made it sound so easy, but Morwena was very dangerous, even to someone as strong as a witch assassin. The lids of that witch's left eye were pinned together with a piece of bone. When she opened it, one glance from that terrible bloodeye could freeze you to the spot. But it was true that she could only use it on one person at a time.

So if we faced her, I hoped she would paralyze me, so that Thorne would be the one to kill her. I didn't want to use the sort of magic it would take to destroy her unless it was absolutely necessary.

Thorne turned to look at me. "So what do we do? Go back, or follow the path around the lake and risk being attacked? You decide, Alice, but do it quickly. You can't stay in the dark much longer without great cost to yourself. And who knows how much time has already passed, out in the world?"

She was right; I couldn't dither. I made up my mind instantly. The thought of retracing my steps filled me with dismay.

"Let's follow the path," I said.

Blades at the ready, Thorne led the way. The path was narrow but dry, the water at least a foot below it.

For the first few minutes we made good progress, although I could see nothing to suggest that the path would lead anywhere significant.

It was then that I noticed the mist that seemed to be forming out in the center of the lake. Tendrils were spreading across its calm surface, meandering toward us.

"Faster!" Thorne cried, having noticed it too. We began to run, but within moments had to slow to a walk again.

The mist was all around us now, so thick that I could hardly make out the shape of Thorne's body even though she was only a couple of paces in front.

To make things worse, the path had suddenly narrowed and become slippery. It was barely higher than the lake now, and in places dipped down so that our pointy shoes were splashing through shallow water.

At any moment I expected Morwena to surge up and attack, but after a tense few moments the path widened out again. Suddenly there were cobbles underfoot, and where my left shoulder and arm had been almost scraping the wall, now it seemed to have receded. There was space to our left, but how much? And if it was veering away from the lake, where did this path lead?

The mist was still thick, so I held my left hand out in front of me to stop myself from blundering into the wall. But as we left the lake, my fear of the water witch slowly abated.

The attack took us by surprise. There wasn't even the faintest warning.

Morwena had not been lurking in the lake. Although she was an entity that rarely ventured far from water, she was waiting for us on dry land.

She appeared out of the mist, standing directly before me. Clawed, webbed feet gripped the cobbles; her skirt and smock were covered in mud and green slime. Her mouth was open, revealing four large yellow fangs, and her flesh-less nose was a sharp triangular bone.

All those things I noted in less than a heartbeat. But then one terrible aspect of her captured my full attention.

Her blood-filled eye was staring directly at me. The bone that pinned it had been removed.

I had gotten my wish. I was now her target.

CHAPTER XXIV

THE THRONE ROOM

I was paralyzed—rooted to the spot. That red, blood-filled eye seemed to grow and grow. I was scared, but one part of me was detached because I had faith in Thorne. It was better this way, better that Morwena had turned her attention on me, if wanted to avoid using my magic.

But suddenly I was aware that

Morwena was not alone. There were other water witches moving up to her side and attacking Thorne, who was now being driven back by the ferocity of that onslaught of fangs and claws.

Morwena took a step toward me, her arms outstretched, ready to rend the flesh from my bones. I was no longer detached; I was terrified. More and more water witches surged past me to attack Thorne. Even her great skill and courage would surely not enable her to defeat so many quickly enough to return and save me.

The foul breath of the powerful witch was now in my face, her fangs ready to bite. I could not think. My mind was paralyzed like my body. I could not summon up any will. Even if I'd wanted to, it was now too late to use my magic. For me, it was over. I had intended to surrender my life for Tom so that he could use my death to destroy the Fiend forever. Now I would die for nothing. Everything that I had done from the moment I was born had been in vain.

Then something happened that I could make no sense of . . .

Something was emerging from Morwena's open mouth.

At first I thought it was some kind of tongue—maybe an aspect of a water witch that I'd never seen before. It was sharp and ridged. It was also covered in blood.

Blood poured from Morwena's mouth, cascading down her chin, and I saw that her bloodeye was no longer looking at me. Both eyes were closed, and she screamed in agony.

Finding that I was now able to move, I quickly stepped back, out of her reach. She twisted away, and in that moment I realized what had happened to her.

A huge skelt had scuttled up onto her back and had transfixed her with its bone tube, driving the tube into the back of her neck so that it had emerged from her mouth. As Morwena staggered and fell forward onto her face, the skelt removed its bone tube and stabbed it into her again, right between the shoulder blades. Immediately the translucent tube turned a bright red as the skelt sucked the blood from her body.

Other witches screamed in anger and ran to her aid, but immediately they had problems of their own. There were more skelts scuttling across the ground, each targeting a water witch.

The mist was lifting, the visibility improving by the second—had it been created by the dark magic of Morwena? It seemed likely. Another skelt scuttled toward me, its thin multijointed legs a blur. It moved so fast that I barely had time to react. It passed by less than an arm's length away but didn't so much as look at me; all its attention was on the slimy witches, who were desperately trying to flee.

"Alice!"

I turned and saw Thorne running toward me, her blades red with blood. Several of the witches were on the ground, each under attack by a skelt.

Thorne pointed toward the stone wall, and I saw a small archway that the mist had hidden from our sight. We ran through it and found ourselves in a large oval antechamber with three narrow passageways leading from it.

Which one led to the throne room? I wondered. Maybe none of them, but anywhere seemed safer than near the water's edge.

"I'll try sniffing them in turn," I told Thorne.

Long-sniffing could sometimes warn of danger. At least I could avoid choosing a passageway that held a direct threat to us. But before I could start, something moved into the chamber behind us.

It was a skelt.

Thorne readied her blades and moved between me and the deadly creature. For a moment it halted and stared at us—perhaps it was already bloated with the blood of the witches and needed no more sustenance. But then, suddenly, it scuttled toward the entrance of the left-hand passageway. There it paused and looked back at us before disappearing from view.

Was it going back the way it had come? If so, others might follow it at any moment, and some of them might still be hungry.

But something very strange happened: The skelt slowly backed out of the passageway until its large red eyes were staring at us once more, then reentered the passageway. We didn't move. I watched the entrance to the chamber in case more skelts came in; Thorne watched the passage the lone skelt had taken.

It was then that the creature backed out into the chamber for the second time. Once more it regarded us with its red eyes—they were exactly the same color as the rubies in the hero swords. . . .

It was strange that the image of a skelt should adorn the hilts of those weapons. I wondered what the connection between them was. Would the Dolorous Blade, the dagger I had come to retrieve, be fashioned in a similar way?

"I think it wants us to follow," I said slowly, trying to make sense of its strange behavior.

"Why would a skelt do that?" Thorne challenged. "If we *were* to follow, the others might follow *us*, and then we'd be trapped between them."

"It might want to lead us to the throne room."

"Why should it help us?"

"Not all creatures of the dark are on the side of the Fiend, are they? They didn't attack *us* just now. They killed the water witches and left us alone."

Thorne looked doubtful. "True, but those skelts in the hot domain weren't exactly friendly. The ones that came out of that boiling lake would have drained our blood for sure if they had caught us."

"Maybe they were just exceptionally hungry. Perhaps the skelts are different here in the Fiend's domain? Maybe they are divided among themselves, just like we witches are? Some are for the Fiend and some against him. Ain't it worth taking a chance? As you keep reminding me, I'm running out of time."

Without even waiting for Thorne's reply, I strode across and entered the passageway. Moments later, I heard her pointy shoes clicking along behind me. We walked in silence for several minutes. At one point the passageway grew very dark, and I pulled the candle stub from my pocket and ignited it with a wish. It was a minor use of magic—better than being unable to see danger ahead. I couldn't hear the skelt ahead of us, but it had to be there.

We emerged into a vast, cavernous space. I held up the candle, but its light was feeble—like a solitary firefly trying to illuminate a dark forest at midnight. At first I could make no sense of what I was seeing. The room was huge, longer than it was wide, and I looked up, suddenly aware of something else. Curtains seemed to be hanging from the arched wooden beams far above.

I realized that finally, after our long search, we had reached the throne room. There was no doubt: The whole purpose of this space was to provide an approach to that throne. There was a path leading toward it, but rather than being covered in marble or carpet, it was formed of grass and flowers.

There was a multitude of flowers with pale yellow petals, which I recognized as primroses. There were daisies, too, and buttercups, and blooms I didn't recognize, all filling the air with a pleasant scent. It seemed strange—more appropriate to Pan's domain than that of the Fiend. I wondered if things were changing here because of the Fiend's absence. But then I heard the drone of insects, and I shuddered, thinking of Beelzebub. Listening more closely, I decided that these sounded more like the gnats and midges of a sleepy summer evening than the bloated bluebottles that had filled my nose and mouth.

No doubt many terrified prisoners had been dragged to this place to suffer the Fiend's cruel wrath, but I'd certainly never been here before.

I began to walk along the grassy path. It was soft and yielding underfoot, with a real spring to it. Directly ahead, I could see the throne itself. It was veiled, partly obscured by those diaphanous curtains that reached almost to the ground. At first I thought it was no more than a dozen paces away. But then I realized my mistake; it was at least ten times farther than that.

I remembered that the Fiend could shift in size. After Old Gregory's battle against the witches on Pendle Hill, the Fiend had tried to destroy Tom, who'd taken refuge in the attic of his brother's farm; that room had been protected by his mam's magic, and the Fiend had been unable to break into it. But afterward, a dark scar had appeared on the southern slope of Hangman's Hill, marking the route he had taken to attack the farm. In the fast fury of his passing, he had felled a huge swathe of trees, showing just how large he had been.

When I encountered the Fiend, he had been perhaps three times the size of a man. But those flattened trees and the size of this throne gave an indication of how truly dreadful he could be. The being who sat here in his fearsome majesty had been big enough to fit a human in his mouth; he'd been much taller than the tallest County tree.

I continued walking forward cautiously, Thorne just behind me. I kept telling myself to be brave. After all, there was no way the Fiend could be here now. His head was still in the sack carried by Grimalkin. He was trapped in that dead flesh.

When I reached the first of the curtains, I came to a halt, and my knees began to tremble. I saw now what it actually was.

It was a web.

"What sort of spider could have made so many huge hanging webs such as these?" I wondered.

It was Thorne who spoke his name.

"It's Raknid."

CHAPTER XXV
THE TESTING

RAKNID and I had met once before, long ago, and his name brought another flood of terrible memories from my time with Lizzie. It had happened the month before she found the leather egg and we encountered Betsy Gammon.

It was at the testing.

"Well, girl," Lizzie had said to me

one morning. "Got something for you to look forward to. In a week's time, on Lammas night, you're for the testing!"

Lammas was one of the four main witch sabbaths—the occasions when the most powerful magic was performed and the Pendle clans were at their most dangerous.

I didn't like the look on Lizzie's face. I knew that every girl trained as a witch had to undergo some sort of ritual called the testing. But the details were never discussed; nothing was passed on from witch to witch.

"But I'm not a Malkin, I'm a Deane!" I protested. "My mother was a Malkin, but my father was a Deane. I'm Alice Deane, so I don't need to be tested."

Lizzie gave me a strange smile. "You're with me and being trained by me, so that makes you a Malkin. You'd better get used to it, girl."

Now, years later, I know why Lizzie smiled so strangely. It turned out later that it was she who was my mother, and I'd been fathered by the Fiend—the Devil himself. But I didn't know that then, so I fell silent. Lizzie often gave weird little smiles; all I was concerned with was the test.

Part of me didn't want to know what the testing involved, but it was always better to be prepared for the worst.

"What will I be tested for?" I asked.

"Two things, girl. First off, to see what type of witchcraft would best suit you—bone magic, blood magic, or familiar magic. Next to find out how strong a witch you're likely to become."

My mouth was really dry now, but I forced myself to ask the next question. "How do they test you? What do they do?"

Lizzie smirked. She was probably enjoying the look of fear on my face. "Best you just wait and see. You'll find out on the night, girl. But in the meantime, there are three things you have to do in order to prepare for the testing. From now on, don't wash. You need a full week of dirt to cake your body so that you'll be ready."

"Why do I need to be dirty?" I asked.

"Dirt and dark magic go together—I thought you knew that. The dirtier the skin, the darker and stronger the magic!

"Secondly, don't eat any meat, not even gravy or soup with a trace of meat in it. And thirdly, think hard about what you'd like to work with as a witch—blood, bone, or a familiar. Because that's one thing you'll have to declare."

I didn't sleep the night before the testing. I was dreading it, and my stomach was in twisty, tormenting knots. Some folk talk about having butterflies when they feel nervous. With me it was more like big fanged snakes and worms were writhing inside me, biting my insides.

I rose at dawn, but that meant I had the whole day to get through before the testing at dusk. I really wanted to wash, but Lizzie had forbidden it, and I was mucky from head to toe, my hair caked with dirt. I kept scratching my itchy head, but that only seemed to make it worse.

Deanes didn't usually go near Malkin Tower. If they got in, they'd most likely never come out alive. There were terrifying stories about bloodstained chambers far beneath it, where the Malkins tortured their enemies before throwing them into deep, dank dungeons to starve to death.

The day passed, and soon we were walking through

Crow Wood, and that dreadful dark stone tower was directly ahead. It was a scary place, all right, at least three times taller than the treetops. It reminded me of a castle tower because of the battlements on top and the narrow pointy windows. It also had a wide moat with a drawbridge. But the big wooden door to the tower was closed. It was studded with rusty iron—a metal that witches could not bear to touch.

Lizzie walked onto the drawbridge, and I followed reluctantly at her heels. Someone waved down to her from the battlements, probably one of the witches from her coven. A moment later we heard heavy bolts being drawn back, and then the door began to swing slowly open, grinding on its hinges. We stepped inside, and the door closed behind us. I stood there, eyes stinging from the smoke that filled the big, gloomy room where the coven lived. I recognized some of their faces because I'd passed them in the village street. But some were complete strangers, and I wondered if they ever left the tower.

By now my mouth was dry, my heart beating against my

ribs fit to burst. Terrible things happened in this tower. I feared that they might happen to me.

In the corners of the room, there were fires with cooking pots—and heaps of bones. Some of these looked like animal bones, but others could easily have been human. Sacks and crumpled dirty sheets lay piled on the floor against the curve of the wall, obviously the witches' beds. In the middle of the room was another fire with a large cauldron bubbling away over it.

The coven stared at me curiously. The witches were dressed in long, dark gowns that looked none too clean, and their faces were streaked with dirt and grease. They stank of stale sweat and animal fat. Lizzie was right: Dirt and dark magic really *did* go together. But there was one tall woman who stood out from the rest, one who looked clean and bright-eyed. Her body was crisscrossed with leather straps, and fastened to them were sheaths holding blades. One weapon wasn't visible, but everybody knew about it. She wore it in a special sheath under her left arm; it was a pair of pointy scissors, which she used to snip off the thumbs of her enemies.

I had never seen her before, but I knew that this witch wasn't a member of the coven of thirteen. She had to be Grimalkin, the assassin of the Malkin clan. Our eyes locked, and she smiled: I saw that behind her black-painted lips, her teeth had been filed to sharp points.

Lizzie seized me by the arm and dragged me toward the far wall, where a big woman with long white hair stood staring at us. I knew her by reputation. It was Maggie Malkin, the leader of the clan.

She scowled at me and took my left arm just above the elbow, squeezing it so hard that I yelped with pain.

"Skinny little thing, ain't she?" Maggie said. "Not much meat on them twiggy bones. Have you told her what happens if she fails the test?"

Lizzie gave me an evil smile. "I thought it best to save that pleasure for you, Maggie. I wouldn't want to steal your thunder!"

It was the first time I'd seen Lizzie being so ingratiating. It made me realize that, as a group, these witches were really powerful. She was nervous of them, no matter what she said about them in private.

With an appreciative nod toward Lizzie, Maggie dragged me toward the big pot in the center of the room. Next to it was a wooden table with several small boxes on it, along with three wooden cups, each covered with a red cloth. Additionally, beside the table stood what looked like a very big box with a black silk cloth laid over it. Maybe it was a chest of drawers? I wondered what was inside.

I tried a sly sniff to see if I could get some hint of what it might be, but I got nothing back. No doubt the coven had collaborated to create a powerful spell to stop nosy people like me.

Two other girls were waiting in the room, looking just as scared as I felt, and Maggie released my arm and pushed me next to them. I knew them by sight, although we'd never spoken. I'd lived with my mam and dad in the Deane village of Roughlee, whereas they were Malkins and came from Goldshaw Booth. The taller girl was called Marsha, the shorter one Gloria.

The coven moved in to encircle us. I could feel Lizzie standing close behind me, her eyes boring into the back of my head.

"Who owns these girls? Who will teach them the craft?" demanded Maggie in a loud voice.

In response I felt Lizzie's hand clamp onto my left shoulder. I kept my eyes straight ahead but knew that two other Malkin witches would have done the same to Marsha and Gloria.

"Three girls I see before me!" cried Maggie. "Three scared girls you be, and there ain't no shame in that. But things are worse than you expect. Ain't no easy way to tell you this, but one of you will die this very night!"

At that, all the witches gave a shriek so fierce and loud that the piles of bones in the corners of the room began to vibrate and spread out across the stone flags.

A tremor of fear ran through me. This was even worse than I'd expected. I'd thought we were about to be tested as a type of witch, not chosen to die. How would they decide which one of us it would be?

Maggie went on to tell us what I already knew from Lizzie: "You'll each be tested twice—firstly, to show us what type of magic would suit you best. The second test will predict your eventual strength as a witch. But then one of you must die so that her strength can be absorbed by the other two. It has always been so. . . . Well, is there anything else you wish to know before the rituals begin?" She glared at each of us in turn.

I didn't think there was any point in asking anything, because it was going to happen anyway, and it might be better not to know in advance. But, to my surprise, Marsha spoke up.

"I know what works for me!" she cried. "Blood is what I need!"

I thought that Maggie would be angry and warn the girl to keep quiet; the coven would surely decide what was best for her. Instead she beamed at her, reached across the table, and lifted one of the wooden cups.

"It's pleasing when a young potential witch knows what's good for her," said Maggie, snatching away the cloth and holding out the cup to the eager Marsha.

I could smell the blood as she lifted it to her lips and began to gulp it down greedily. It was human blood, too—I could smell it, and I wondered where they'd gotten it. Had someone been murdered to provide what they needed? Maybe it was the blood of some prisoner they kept in the dungeons below the tower.

It disgusted me to watch her slurp it. So eager was Marsha to drain the cup that blood trickled down out of the corners of her mouth and began to drip from the end of her chin. With a satisfied smile she handed the cup back to Maggie, who placed it on the table, then picked up the second cup and handed it to the smaller girl, Gloria.

I could tell by the look on Gloria's face that she didn't fancy even a sip of what that wooden cup contained. She tried, I'll give her that. First she held her nose with the thumb and forefinger of her right hand. She brought the cup to her lips twice, each time holding it away again at arm's length, gagging. Finally she managed to take a sip, but then she heaved. Blood mixed with vomit spurted out of her mouth to splash down on the floor between her and the witch.

Maggie wasn't best pleased, and she gave the poor girl a furious glare before snatching the cup from her hand. Then she offered the third cup to me, but I folded my arms and shook my head.

"I ain't a blood witch," I told her. "I can sniff it from here, and it's not for me."

"You'll try it, girl, if you know what's good for you," Maggie warned. "If you don't try it, we'll force it down your throat."

I knew they'd do just that, so reluctantly I took a small sip. It was cold, salty, and had a metallic tang. There was no way I was going to swallow that, so I spat it out and shook my head again. For a moment I thought Maggie was going to carry out her threat and force me to drink the whole amount, but she frowned, snatched the cup away, and put it on the table before opening one of the small boxes and taking something from it.

"Hold out your left hand, girl." She strode over to face

me again. I could see that she was holding a pair of thumb bones. She placed them in the palm of my left hand.

"Grip 'em tightly and tell me who they belonged to and how their owner died."

It was something I'd often practiced with Lizzie. I had learned to tell a lot from just touching a bone.

I did as instructed, and shivered immediately. They were as cold as ice. Instantly the images of a terrible murder flashed into my head. A priest was walking down a narrow woodland track toward a bridge over a fast-flowing stream. It was dark, but a thin crescent moon dappled the ground with shadows of twigs and leaves. He turned to glance back down the track, and I saw his eyes widen with fear. He was being followed by witches.

The priest began to run. If only he could reach the stream, he'd be safe, because witches couldn't cross running water. But he was too old to run quickly, and they caught him easily. There were three witches, and I recognized two of them: one was Maggie, the other Lisa Dugdale—a sour-faced witch who didn't know what a smile was. They held him down, and he began to scream as they cut his thumbs away while he was still alive. He had a large chalice in his bag, and they used that to collect his blood. Then they threw his body into the river, and it was carried away downstream by the torrent. The last thing I saw was his sightless eyes staring up at the moon.

I suddenly realized that he had been killed only the previous night. Not only was I holding his thumb bones, from which the flesh had been boiled less than an hour ago; it was his blood that I'd been forced to drink.

"Well, girl, what have you learned?" demanded Maggie.

"The bones belong to an old farmer," I said. "He was gored by a bull. While he was dying, a witch came and collected his thumb bones."

I'd lied because there was no way I was ever going to become a bone witch. They murdered people to get the bones they used in magic rituals; many of those were only children. I would never do that.

"Rubbish!" Maggie snapped, and took the bones from me and handed them to Gloria, whose eyes rolled up into her head the moment they touched them. Her teeth chattered and she began to shiver and tremble all over.

"They're the bones of a dead priest! Didn't like his blood, but love his old bones!" she cried.

Maggie grinned. "They're yours, girl. Keep 'em. You'll become a bone witch, for sure. But what are we going to do with you, Alice Deane?" she demanded. "Only one thing left. Fail that, and you can't be a witch at all. And if you can't be a witch, you might as well be dead. So that's what will happen!"

She went across and lifted another small box from the table. Maggie opened it, then stooped and shook something out onto the floor at my feet. "This could be your first familiar, girl. Let's see if he likes you."

I looked down, horrified, at what was twitching on the ground no more than a hand's breadth from my foot.

I'd had a fear of creepy-crawlies for just about as long as I could remember. Sometimes as a young child I'd had nightmares in which I was trapped in my bed, staring up at the bedroom ceiling, which was covered in spiders' webs. I'd be in mortal terror, lying paralyzed on my back, waiting for the big spider to appear.

And this was just about the biggest, hairiest spider I'd ever seen. This type of spider didn't belong in the County, so it had to be from overseas. Either that, or it was specially crafted using dark magic. Looked like it could bite. Might even be poisonous.

A familiar witch made a pact with a creature. She fed it her blood, and in return it became her eyes and ears and did her bidding. Having a familiar was better than being a blood or a bone witch, but although I might have coped with a cat or maybe some kind of bird, I feared and hated spiders.

After Lizzie had told me about the testing, I'd been worrying about it a lot and had decided that if I had to choose a type of magic, familiar would be best, and the animal I might cope with best would be a cat.

"A spider ain't my choice of familiar!" I cried. "I need a cat. That's what suits me!"

"You'll do as you're told, girl!" Maggie snapped. "You

need to start off small. You train using a spider 'cause they don't live long. Maybe later you can have a cat."

I stared in horror at the spider. Just the thought of it touching me made me shudder.

It scuttled toward me.

What if it ran up my skirt . . . ?

I acted without thought. I just did what I had to do.

I stepped forward and squashed that nasty spider with the toe of my pointy left shoe, smearing it into the floor.

As I stepped back, the air was filled with cries of outrage. I looked at the angry faces staring at me, and even now I remember that just one was different. Just one face wasn't contorted with anger.

Grimalkin was smiling.

Maggie stepped toward me, then slapped me hard across the face, bringing tears to my eyes. Next she dragged me across to the table by my hair and picked up a knife.

"She has defiled the testing. Another must replace her. Is this girl fit to be a witch of the Malkin clan?" she demanded.

"Unfit! Unfit! Unfit!" the coven chanted in unison, until

the piles of bones began to vibrate and rattle.

"Does she deserve to die? Shall I kill her now?" Maggie cried.

I looked back at Lizzie. Her face was hard to read, and she wasn't chanting with her sisters, but she had bowed her head slightly, as if in deference to the will of the coven. I could expect no help from her.

"Kill her! Kill! Kill! Kill!" yelled the coven members, ending their chant with a chorus of shrieks.

Maggie raised the knife above her head and prepared to stab down into my chest. I closed my eyes, feeling sick to my stomach.

I was going to die.

CHAPTER XXVI
THE STRONG ONES

"STOP now!" a lone voice cried out in a commanding tone. I opened my eyes and watched Grimalkin step out of the circle and approach Maggie.

"You dare too much!" Maggie hissed. "By her behavior the girl has forfeited her life."

I glanced at Lizzie, whose eyes had widened in astonishment.

"She is just a child and has much to learn," said Grimalkin, easing the hilt of a dagger from its sheath so that the sharp metal of the blade gleamed in the firelight. "To take her life might waste a rare talent. She has courage and deserves to move on to the second test. Let's see just how strong she could become."

Maggie tightened her grip on my hair. "The clan has voted for her death. As leader, I have a mandate to slay her. The testing has been defiled. We will kill the girl and convene again at the next sabbath for a new testing."

Grimalkin eased her dagger another inch or so from its scabbard and took another step toward Maggie. She was balanced on her toes, coiled like a spring, ready to attack. A deadly, expectant silence fell upon the gathering.

"Clan leaders can be replaced," hissed Grimalkin. Then her eyes swept around the circle of witches. "So can this coven!"

I saw the fear in the eyes of the witches. Some stepped back; one eyed the door as if calculating her chances of escape. They were all clearly scared of Grimalkin—even

Lizzie. I had thought that the assassin was controlled by the coven and did its bidding without question. The balance of power here was not what I'd expected.

"You speak nonsense. Nothing has been defiled. Continue with the testing. Let Raknid decide," continued Grimalkin, her tone more conciliatory. "If he marks this girl for death, then I will accept that choice."

I wondered who Raknid was. I looked around quickly but could see no men in the room. The coven had male servants too, but none seemed to be present at this meeting.

Maggie let out a sigh, released my hair, and stepped back. "Very well. We would be foolish to quarrel about this child. It will soon be settled one way or the other. We will move on to the second test."

Grimalkin nodded, sheathed her blade, and stepped back to join the circle of witches. I caught Lizzie's eye, and she beckoned to me. I obeyed her and moved back to my original position.

I was grateful for Grimalkin's intervention—she'd saved my life. But why had she done it? I had no opportunity to think further about it, because it was time for the second part of the test.

Maggie looked at us each in turn. "For now, the three of you still live. But death moves closer with each second that passes. Now I will summon Raknid, the tester. He will assess your strengths and select the one who will die."

"Who's Raknid?" Marsha asked.

I thought Maggie would refuse to answer, but Marsha was clearly her favorite.

"There was once a dangerous boggart that folk called the Pendle Ripper. It was used by our clan to attack our enemies. It was formidable, killing more than a hundred of them over less than forty years. Outsiders assume it is dead or dormant, but seventy years ago, by use of powerful dark magic, we elevated that boggart to the level of a demon. He still does our bidding, but spends most of his time in the dark, only entering our world when summoned. His main task is to assess new witches and decide which of the three should surrender her strength and life to the others."

I felt really annoyed at Lizzie. Surely she could have given me a bit of warning about what was to happen tonight? My life was at risk, yet I'd walked into the tower like a lamb to the slaughter.

Maggie strode toward the big box beside the table and pulled off the black cloth that covered it. As she folded it, placing it carefully on the table, my eyes were drawn to the large object that had been revealed. I had expected some sort of wooden box, but this was crafted from metal. It stood upon four iron legs carved into the shape of scaly feet, each with three sharp-clawed toes. It was a square cabinet, its top made of glass, with a small circular hole right at its center.

What was that for? I wondered.

At a signal from Maggie, the coven began to chant again. I recognized it as a spell of summoning. They were calling the demon.

The air grew cold very quickly, and I began to shiver. I thought I heard a distant rumble of thunder, but then realized that the sound was coming from somewhere below. Was it something down in the dungeons?

Soon the floor started to shake and the tower itself seemed to move. There was a roar, like the warning cry of some fierce animal, and the metal cabinet began to vibrate. Then, suddenly, everything became very still and silent again.

There was dangerous dark magic being deployed here. I was scared about what might happen next. Were any of us safe from such a powerful entity?

"Raknid is here," Maggie announced, "and is ready to begin the testing. You shall be first. Come here, child!"

Maggie was pointing at Gloria, and the girl walked forward to stand beside the clan leader, who put a hand on her shoulder and led her right up to the metal cabinet.

"Put your hand in the cabinet palm upward, girl, and leave it there. But before you do so, look upon Raknid."

Gloria looked down through the glass, and I saw her eyes widen. "No," she murmured. "Please . . . I don't want to do it."

"You have no choice, girl. Every witch in our clan has

endured this. You must put your hand into the cabinet. And don't try to remove it until I give you permission. Remove it earlier, and you'll be without a hand for the rest of your life. Understand?"

Gloria nodded and, very slowly and reluctantly, put her hand through the circular hole. Within seconds she was shrieking like a piglet about to have its throat cut.

Hearing her scream like that made me tremble all over. What was in that cabinet? Soon my hand would be inside it.

After about thirty seconds, Maggie told Gloria to pull her hand out of the hole, and she returned to her place, clasping it against her side. Blood was dripping from it— the demon had clearly bitten her. Drawing blood was no doubt part of the process of testing.

Next it was the turn of Marsha. She came forward with a confident look on her face, but when she peered down through the glass into the cabinet, I saw fear distort her features too, and her knees began to tremble. What was the form taken by the demon? It had to be something really scary.

But whatever it looked like and whatever the pain,

Marsha was far braver than Gloria. She cried out just once, and then became silent as the demon did its work. All too soon it was my turn to be beckoned forward.

"This couldn't be better, Alice Deane," the clan leader told me. "There is a certain justice here after what you did before. Look down!"

I peered down through the glass and immediately began to shiver with fear. The demon had taken on the shape of a gigantic, hairy spider. Its body was the size of a human head, each of its eight legs as long as my forearm.

It had once been a boggart, before becoming more powerful and transforming into a demon. Hairy boggarts usually took on the shape of cats, dogs, goats, or horses. I had never heard of one looking like a spider. It was rare, and probably very dangerous.

"Put your left hand into the cabinet, girl!" Maggie commanded. "Palm upward."

I began to sweat and shake. I feared all creepy-crawlies, and spiders were at the top of the list. This was a nightmare. How could I do it?

But Maggie had come close to killing me. If I refused now, I would forfeit my life. Even Grimalkin would be unable to save me.

It took all my willpower to force my body to obey. Slowly and nervously, with a dry mouth, I put my hand through the hole toward the huge, terrifying spider.

Despite my fear, I was determined not to let it show. I would not cry out in pain. Why give 'em that satisfaction?

The spider placed one of its hairy legs across my wrist. I shuddered at its touch. The leg felt very heavy, and I knew it was pinning down my hand so that I couldn't move it. When the creature opened its mouth, it took all my strength not to scream, for it had the long, curved, poisonous fangs of a snake.

It bit down quickly into the soft mound of flesh below my thumb. I groaned, but somehow managed not to cry out. The pain was severe. It felt as if two hot needles were pressing deeper and deeper into my flesh. Then the blood began to flow, forming a red pool in the palm of my hand. It seemed to go on for many minutes—much longer than what the other two girls had had to endure—but at last Maggie told me to withdraw my hand.

I didn't hold it against my dress as the other two had. What was the point of that? I'd only struggle to get the stains out afterward—that's if I survived the night. I just let it fall to my side and returned to my place by Lizzie, leaving a trail of blood on the flags.

A voice boomed from the cabinet, making the piles of bones vibrate again. It was harsh and rasping, like the teeth of a coarse file grinding against jagged metal.

"The weakest is the girl Gloria. Her bone magic will hardly be worth the name. She'd make a better servant than a witch—more suited to cooking and cleaning. As for Marsha, she is thrice as strong and will become a powerful blood witch. The most powerful of all by far, however, is the girl Alice. All she needs is a suitable familiar."

I saw Maggie's face twist with anger, and the other witches gave gasps of surprise. Maggie had wanted me to be the weakest and Marsha to be the strongest—I was sure of it. But I felt sorry for poor Gloria. As the declared weakest, she would be the one to forfeit her life. As for what he'd said about me, I was surprised. I was a reluctant trainee witch and didn't think I'd any special aptitude for the craft—I didn't *want* to be good at it.

But the demon hadn't finished yet. "Although she is the strongest, Alice must forfeit her life now. I sense danger. One day she may become an enemy of the dark. Better safe than sorry, so take her strength now and share it between the other two!"

"That ain't fair!" I cried out—arguing my own case for the first time. "I've passed the test and beaten the other two! I'm the strongest. Why should I die?"

"Shut your face, girl! Raknid has spoken, and the tester's word is law. Even Grimalkin will abide by it. Is that not so?" Maggie asked, looking at the witch assassin.

I turned toward Grimalkin, hoping against hope that she might intervene again, but she simply compressed her lips and gave the faintest of nods.

So next I turned back to plead with Lizzie. "Help me!" I cried. "How can this be right when I'm the strongest?"

"I can do nothing, girl. The law is the law."

Nobody would help me now. This was it.

I thought they were going to give me to Raknid, but to my surprise the witches began to chant again. Once more the metal cabinet began to vibrate, and the room grew steadily warmer. When the spell was completed, there was a feeling of peace and calm. Raknid was gone. The demon had returned to the dark.

"Bring the girl here!" Maggie commanded, and Lizzie pushed me toward her.

To my surprise, there was a sad expression on the clan leader's face. "I've done this many times, girl," she said, "and I know you must be afraid, so I'd like to offer you a few words of comfort. First of all, I can promise you it won't hurt much. There'll be a pressure inside your head, and then you'll fall away into soothing darkness and the pain of this life will be over.

"Next, I want you to think how you'll be helping your clan, so your death won't be in vain. Two other young witches, Marsha and Gloria, will receive your strength and be better able to serve our needs. And you have a lot of power to yield, so remember that. You leave a legacy, girl. Be glad to serve us."

I glanced across at Lizzie. It wasn't that I expected any help, because she'd told me plainly that she could do nothing to oppose clan law. But I thought she might at least be a bit sad that I was going to die, even a little annoyed because of the time she'd wasted in training me. But her face was a mask—no trace of emotion—and her eyes were like two black coals.

"It ain't right!" I shouted. "What do I care about you lot? My life's not even worth tuppence to you. I'll be dead!"

"Being dead's not that bad," Maggie told me. "We'll carry your body to Witch Dell and bury it there in a shallow grave under the rotting leaves. You'll be nice and cozy, and when the first beam of the full moon falls on your grave, you'll come back to life and be able to go hunting for victims. Dead witches really love the taste of blood. And there are so many delicious flavors—rats, mice, rabbits, even humans, if you manage to catch one."

"You're lying!" I screeched. "That only happens to dead witches, and I ain't a witch yet. I'll just fall into the dark and you know it!"

Maggie didn't reply. She knew what I'd said was true.

I turned and ran toward the big door, but then realized I had no hope of getting away because it was barred. It would have taken me several minutes to draw every bar across, and even then I probably wouldn't have had the strength to open that heavy door by myself; the drawbridge was most likely raised as well. But I wasn't even thinking then. I was desperate, like a frightened animal in a trap when the gamekeeper comes to collect it.

The witches caught me easily and brought me back to stand before Maggie. My hands were bound behind my back, and I was forced to my knees before her. I felt numb; I couldn't believe this was happening to me. Memories of my childhood flitted through my mind. I saw my mam and dad rolling on the floor, fighting; he was trying to throttle her while she was scratching at his eyes with her long nails. But there were happier ones, too: walking through the woods alone, just listening to the birds. My life had hardly begun, though. I'd hoped that somehow it would start to get better, but it was just going to end here in Malkin Tower.

There was nothing I could do to save myself. They had made up their minds, and I wasn't strong enough to fight them all.

I was held in position by two witches while Gloria and Marsha each placed a hand on my left shoulder. Then Maggie put her hands on top of my head and exerted a steady pressure, beginning the singsong chant that would draw forth my strength and life into the bodies of the two girls, leaving me stone-dead on the flags.

At first I struggled, but then I felt the beginnings of pain: a slow pressure building right inside my head. The pain grew until I thought my head would burst. Now I could hardly think. All that was left was emotion—a mixture of anger and resentment.

Why should I die while Marsha and Gloria lived? I thought. It wasn't fair!

I must have screamed, or maybe I just cried out in anger. The next thing I knew, the hands had released their grip on my body, and Maggie had fallen away.

I lurched to my feet. Maggie was lying on her back, her whole body twitching. Her eyes had rolled right up into her head, and she was spitting out small pieces of tooth, vomit dribbling from her mouth. The two witches who had held me down were on their knees, cradling their hands against their bodies, their faces twisted in pain. The two girls were sobbing.

I looked about me and saw eyes staring at me in horror. What had happened? But once again, Grimalkin was smiling. She stepped forward to seize my arm, and then turned and spoke to Lizzie.

"The girl is free to go," she said. "Another life must be forfeit."

Lizzie nodded and smiled back. Within moments my hands had been released; the big doors of Malkin Tower were opened and the drawbridge lowered. Astonished, I walked out into the fresh air with Grimalkin at my side.

Lizzie was following at our heels. I couldn't believe it was over and I was still alive.

On the drawbridge, the witch assassin leaned close to my left ear.

"I would have stood on that spider too, Alice," she whispered. "That's what we do. We are the strong ones. We squash anything that we don't like. Anything that threatens us gets smeared!"

All the way home, Bony Lizzie refused to answer my questions, but back at the cottage she finally relented.

"Will they still come for me?" I asked. "Will I still have to die?"

Lizzie shook her head. "No, girl, you're safe for now. Maggie wasn't strong enough to suck away your power. So she paid the price. When she's well enough, one of the other girls will have to die in your place. It will be Gloria, as she is the weakest."

"Why couldn't Maggie do it?" I asked. "Why couldn't she take my power?"

"Who knows?" said Lizzie, giving me a strange smile.

"But the witch who takes another's power must be stronger than her victim. Otherwise she pays a hefty price."

"Are you saying that I'm somehow stronger than Maggie?" I asked in amazement.

"Not yet, girl, so don't get ideas above your station. There's a lot of work in front of you yet. But you must have the potential—otherwise Maggie wouldn't have suffered that attack."

CHAPTER XXVII
THE SPIDER DEMON

I still remembered my own testing as if it had happened yesterday—how I had crushed that spider beneath the heel of my pointy shoe; how I had been forced to place my hand in the glass-topped cabinet and let Raknid, the spider demon, bite me. Afterward he had said I was the strongest of the three girls. . . .

393

Raknid's words had indeed proved to be correct. I was the enemy of the Fiend and his servants, and that now meant that Raknid was my enemy. If he had his way, I would die here.

But not if I could help it! I was strong, and I would do what was necessary.

"Look! Up there!" cried Thorne, pointing to something almost directly above us. It was the skelt that had led us here. It seemed to be writhing, legs twitching, twisting, spinning, suspended from what appeared to be a rope.

No . . . it wasn't a rope. The creature was bound fast by a silken thread spun from the demon's body, still out of sight, high above us. And now the skelt was being hauled aloft. I watched it being pulled higher and higher into the darkness of the roof, where the light of my candle couldn't reach, up into the place where the spider demon was waiting to feed.

The creature had paid a terrible price for guiding us to the throne room.

"Perhaps Raknid is too occupied with the skelt to notice us," Thorne suggested.

But there was no conviction in her voice. We both knew the truth.

Raknid would know we were here. He would feed quickly, drain the skelt, and then we would be next on the menu. To escape from the throne room, we would have to fight him head-on.

"Let's find the blade and get out of here," I said, hurrying toward the gigantic throne.

But the nearer we got, the less I liked what I saw. The throne was raised up on a base that was set above the grassy path. We could walk underneath it and search without having to stoop. It seemed almost too easy. Was it a trap? Was there something else here, in addition to the spider demon? No sooner had that thought entered my head than I glimpsed something moving under the throne. There were eyes reflected in the gleam of the candle flame.

I stepped beneath the Fiend's throne, the candle held

before me, Thorne at my shoulder. But then I saw that there were lots of eyes belonging to different large insects. Some of them were huge. The nearest one looked like a centipede and had a long undulating body the thickness of my arm.

More scary creepy-crawlies . . .

Then a further horror was revealed by the light of the candle.

All these creatures had human faces.

The centipede spoke, its voice hardly more than the rustle and crackle of dry dead leaves stirred by the wind. But somehow it communicated extreme sadness.

"Once we walked the earth with human bodies," it explained. "We served the Fiend on earth but eventually displeased him. This is our punishment—to take these shapes and crawl for all eternity beneath his throne. There are others like us who live in the vaults beneath the basilica, and also in some of the deepest cellars of the city. We hate to be gazed upon. Depart from here, and leave us to suffer."

The creature squinted toward the candle flame, and its eyes began to water.

Thorne's own eyes widened in astonishment and pity, and it was left to me to reply.

"We will leave as soon as we can," I replied. "But first we must search for something. There is a dagger hidden beneath this throne. Show us where it is, and we will be away at once."

None of those pitiful creatures replied; instead, so accustomed to darkness that they were dazzled by the feeble light of my candle, they turned and fled.

Without a word, Thorne and I began to search the grassy area beneath the throne. Where could the dagger be?

It might be hidden in the grass; this was no longer the fragrant, flower-filled carpet that had led from the door to the throne. It was sodden and stank of rot, so that our shoes squelched with each step, and it was covered with disgusting debris—dead skin shed by the creatures that had fled, along with coarse hair and warty protuberances. I avoided touching it with my hand and just pushed everything aside with my shoes.

We completed our searches at the same time. We'd found nothing.

"Perhaps it's buried in the ground?" Thorne suggested.

Were we going to have to dig up the whole area under the throne? I wondered.

"The blade could be anywhere," I said. "What if it's already been moved? If Morwena knew we were coming here to get it, she could have taken it."

Then, suddenly, I had a sinking feeling in the pit of my stomach. "There's someone else who could have hidden it," I murmured.

Thorne nodded. "You mean Raknid? Yes, I think that's very likely."

Together we emerged from beneath that immense throne and gazed upward. The skelt was no longer visible. Strands of the web were fastened to the walls and various parts of the floor, each one thicker than my forefinger; there were even a couple attached high on the throne.

I held the candle up as far as I could. It illuminated the

lower edge of the central part of the web. The web had been constructed on a vast scale, and there were things stuck to it, desiccated, long-dead things—Raknid's victims.

But they were not the flies you might find in an ordinary spider's web.

These had arms and legs; heads, too.

They were human.

"If I were Raknid, I'd bind the blade high up in my web so that anyone seeking it would have to climb up to reach it," said Thorne.

"That's what I have to do," I realized.

I was afraid, but I hadn't come all this way and gone through so much to fail now.

Thorne pointed at the nearest strand of web and shook her head. "It's sticky—you'd get bound to it. And the moment you touch it, the web will vibrate, alerting the spider demon. His feet won't stick to the web like yours. He'll scuttle across and inject you with venom. You'll be paralyzed. Then he'll tug you up into the darkness and start to feed on you. You'll be conscious all the time, and you'll be in agony. He won't just take your blood. He'll suck the brains from your skull. He'll drain every bit of fluid from your body until you're just a dry, dead husk. Don't you see? He *wants* you to climb it. So don't do it, Alice. There has to be another way."

Then, as if he had been listening to every word we'd uttered, Raknid spoke to us from the darkness above, his deep, harsh voice vibrating through my head and setting my teeth on edge.

"Yes, climb up to me, little witch! Let's see how brave you really are. Don't listen to your cowardly dead friend. What does she know? I have the Dolorous Blade that you seek. Are you brave enough to try and take it from me?"

"*I'll* climb up and confront him!" said Thorne furiously. "I will stick to his web, but when he attacks he'll find me no easy prey. This blade will take out his eyes!"

"Wait for a moment. Let me speak to him first." I held Thorne's arm to prevent her from climbing the nearest strand up into the web.

A slow anger began to build within me. Back in Malkin

Tower, this demon had taken my blood and then condemned me to death. Now I would not only take the blade; I would pay Raknid back for what he had done.

"I think you lie!" I shouted up into the dark. "I don't believe you have the blade."

"Why would I lie? The blade is here with me."

"Then show it to me! *Prove* that you have it. Why should I climb up there for nothing?"

"For a little witch, you have caused us big trouble. I knew that when I tasted your blood. You are strong for a mere girl, and in your prime might have become peerless; but you will not survive to fulfill your potential. I was right about the danger I sensed within you. You are a grave threat to my master. But I will show you the blade, because I know it will bring you to my side! And then I will kill you!"

Suddenly the huge web trembled. Raknid had probably been crouching on a ledge far above. Now he had stepped onto the threads, causing them to shake. He was climbing down toward us. Within seconds he was taking up a position at the very center of his web.

He was huge—far larger than he'd been in the metal cabinet in Malkin Tower. The rounded central part of his body, which was covered in long, silky red-brown hair, was perhaps the size of a bull, but his eight long, thin black legs tripled his size.

And there at his side was a dagger, stuck to the web.

"I see a blade!" I cried. "But how do I know it's Dolorous? Ain't no way to tell from this distance, is there? Bring it nearer so that I can be sure!"

"No, little witch. You must climb up to me!"

I leaned across to whisper into Thorne's ear: "When he falls, be ready to slay him."

Her eyes widened in astonishment.

Then I ran forward and held the flame of my candle against the nearest strand of the web. It smoldered a little, but the strand remained intact. It did not catch fire.

The candle flickered and was about to go out.

"You fool!" Raknid laughed.

But I was no fool; just desperate enough to do what had

to be done. I was gathering my power. That was the reason for the delay. I did not speak a word. I didn't need spells—though I knew there might be a price to pay later.

I remembered the warning that Agnes Sowerbutts had once given me regarding my use of magic: "You can't use that power for anyone or anything, or it will destroy you. It comes from the very heart of darkness, and if you use it willy-nilly as you've just done, it will seize you for its own and take your soul."

But I had to risk it.

So I simply wished . . . and it was done.

The candle flame grew brighter, caught, then raced up the web strand directly toward the spider demon.

For a second Raknid didn't react. Perhaps he couldn't believe what was happening . . .

The whole web went up in a *whoosh* of flame, yellow and orange, so bright that it hurt my eyes.

Raknid was burning too. He was burning and shrieking—so shrilly that it was like sharp needles being driven into my ears. His red fur was crisping to black.

Now he was falling. Falling like a meteorite plummeting to earth.

But the dagger was falling faster.

Like a hawk stooping to a falconer's wrist, the Dolorous Blade came straight to my hand.

I caught it by the handle and tossed it toward Thorne.

Over and over it spun, end over end, and she caught it too.

"Kill him!" I commanded.

Raknid, still shrieking, hit the ground in a shower of sparks.

Thorne went to work quickly.

He fell silent.

Then we ran.

CHAPTER XXVIII
POOR BRAVE THORNE

T HE first time we paused to catch our breath, I examined the dagger carefully. It resembled the other one needed for the ritual. The sword and the daggers were of different lengths, but the hilts were identical, with their skelt heads and ruby-red eyes. But this was the Dolorous Blade—the one that would be used to take my life.

Then, as I held that dagger, a wave of sadness passed through me. It was like nothing I'd ever experienced before. It wasn't simply that it was linked to my own approaching death; it was as if I was suddenly connected to the sadness of millions of souls. I staggered and almost dropped the blade, and Thorne held my arm to steady me.

"Are you all right? Are you ill?" she asked anxiously.

I saw no point in telling her what I had experienced, so I just smiled. "I'm tired, that's all. We must move on. I have to leave this place."

So we set off again. It took a long time to sniff out the gate, hours and hours of searching. All the time I was scared, and very much aware that we were being hunted down by powerful beings.

And our enemies had lots of reasons to try and stop us.

Thorne had hurt Beelzebub and killed Tusk; we had fought the water witches and had been there when Morwena was slain. We had destroyed the demon Raknid. And now we were escaping with the Dolorous Blade, one of the three hero swords that could be used to destroy the Fiend.

They would do anything to catch us.

But at last we found the gate and passed through it safely. We found ourselves once more on the white path that crossed the black abyss, joining domain to domain.

It was then, just as we were approaching a cave, that the demon Tanaki found us.

In the blink of an eye, with a sound of thunder, the father of the kretch arrived.

He was a colossus—far too big to fit into the cave—but he materialized between us and our refuge. I had come so close, but now our chance of escape was gone.

Whether Tanaki was floating or standing on something far below the path was impossible to say, but he straddled it, his legs level with our heads, while his head and body towered above us. He was a fearsome sight and, like his son, there was much that was wolflike about him.

His hairy jaw was elongated, and large, pointed canines jutted upward and downward, too big to fit inside. He opened his mouth and roared, his hot, rank breath rushing over us like scalding steam, so that I was forced to shield my eyes with my forearm. I could easily fit within that mouth; I was no more than a morsel for such a monster, chewed and swallowed in an instant.

Once again Thorne stepped between me and the threat. She was brave and dangerous, but what chance did she have?

She was already sliding a dagger from its sheath. But the demon was not only huge; he was very fast. He struck down at Thorne with a scaly taloned hand. She somersaulted backward, but Tanaki delivered a glancing blow to her shoulder and spun her onto the stones.

He gripped both sides of the path with his monstrous hands, mouth wide open, ready to crunch Thorne in his jaws.

I had to do something.

But did I dare use my magic one more time?

Surely I had almost reached the point of no return. . . .

CHAPTER XXIX
HEART OF DARKNESS

EVERY time I used my magical power, the crescent mark on my thigh had grown bigger and bigger; it was now close to becoming a full moon.

The blood jar that I had used to keep the Fiend away from Tom had seemed to make little difference. But in Ireland, I had used my power to save him from death. So much magical energy had surged out of me that it had caused a localized earthquake. I had saved our lives, but when I next checked my mark, it had become a half-moon.

Then, soon after Thorne's death, I had used my magic to help Grimalkin retrieve the Fiend's head from his supporters. They had been about to set sail for Ireland, where they would have reunited head and body, returning the Fiend to his former state, loose in the world. I had used my magic to conjure up a storm and burn their ship. With my help, Grimalkin had eventually triumphed, but the cost to me had been terrible. Even before the burning of the spider demon Raknid, the mark on my thigh had grown to a gibbous moon. Afterward I hadn't even dared glance at it, fearful of what might be revealed. Further expenditure of magic might make it a full circle. Then I would belong to the dark forever.

Poor, brave Thorne had died a horrible death on earth, her thumbs cut away by the dark mage Bowker on the edge of Witch Dell. Now she faced a second death in the jaws of the demon Tanaki.

How could I allow that, after all she had done to help me?

But how could I use my magic again when I knew what the result might be?

My knees were trembling and my heart threatened to pound itself out of my chest. But I forced myself to step forward until I was between Thorne and that monstrous mouthful of savage, vengeful teeth.

I wasn't going to use my magic carelessly, was I? I wasn't going to use it to keep me dry in a rainstorm or make branches bow away out of my path as I had on my walk back to Pendle to see Agnes. I was going to use it to fight the demon Tanaki. I was doing it for Thorne.

"Get back!" I cried, raising my fists at the demon. "Leave her be! You can't have her!"

For a moment the huge head paused. I saw the hungry expression in the bestial eyes change quickly, revealing three things: humor, anger, and finally contempt.

It was the last of these that brought the fury rising up like bile in my throat.

"You don't know who I am!" I screamed up at him. "You don't know who I *really* am!"

The demon's mocking laughter rumbled across the abyss. Tanaki was amused by my outburst.

Then I spoke again—this time quietly, words whispering from my lips as if uttered by another.

"I am Alice," I announced. "And you ain't strong enough to stand against me!"

If I could burn Raknid, I could do the same to Tanaki.

I had no choice. Whatever it cost me, this must be done.

My anger became fire. I shuddered with ecstasy as it left my body, surging through my shoulders and arms to exit through my clenched fists. The two jets of white flame hit their targets simultaneously—the eyes of the demon.

I stood swaying, almost floating up from the path, so extreme was my sense of exultation. The demon was screaming now, his eyes melting and running down his cheeks. Then, like a huge tree felled by a woodsman's ax, he slowly toppled sideways and fell away into the abyss.

I turned, dragging Thorne to her feet. She seemed

befuddled and stared at me with wide eyes. She opened her mouth to speak, but no words came out. I seized her arm, and she leaned against me as we stumbled along the path to the shelter of the cave. Once there, she shrugged me off, so I tugged the candle out of my pocket again, ignited it with my will, and led the way farther into the darkness.

Three times we entered cave systems and located gates that took us elsewhere. Once we ended up in a place of ice and snow, and would have died had not the exit gate been close by. Once we reentered the hot domain where the skelts had scuttled out of the boiling lake. But we had been there before; the gate was still in the same place. We got out quickly, but I was starting to feel exhausted.

Finally we emerged into a domain of total darkness; we could hear the roar of huge predators and the *thump-thump* of their gigantic feet getting nearer.

It was a close thing, but we found the gate before they found us.

Something was really starting to worry me. I was feeling weaker and weaker. Thorne had told me that being in

the dark while still alive would use up my life force, that if
I stayed too long, I would end up a dried husk, able to live
for only a few days once back on earth.

I needed to get out of the dark as soon as possible.

Was it already too late for me?

Now we were on the white path again; it disappeared
directly ahead into a cave at the base of a huge black cliff.
Thorne felt certain that this would lead to the domain of
Pan. Beyond that the outside world awaited me—the land
of the living.

We were almost there.

I was almost home.

Almost safe . . .

After a few minutes, Thorne put her hand on my shoulder. "Let's rest for a while. I want to talk," she said.

I was feeling shaky and was only too glad to stop, so we
sat down cross-legged, facing each other, and I placed the
flickering candle between us.

"How did you do that to the demon?" Thorne asked.

My reply was a shrug.

"Raknid too," she continued. "You burned his web and brought him to the ground in flames. And the dagger flew into your hands as if it had wings. Mine was the easy part. All I had to do was finish him off. Grimalkin told me you had powerful magic, but I didn't expect that. I've never seen such power used by a witch."

"Is that the end of Tanaki?" I said, trying to change the subject.

"Things are hard to predict here," Thorne replied, "but I think it's unlikely. As I told you, if something that was born and died back on earth is killed here for a second time, it ceases to exist; the soul is obliterated. So the kretch has likely fallen to his second and final death. Morwena too is gone forever. But Tanaki is different; like his son, he has great powers of regeneration. If he survived the fall, he could eventually get his eyes back. And once set on a course, he never deviates until his will is accomplished; any defeat only makes him stronger. Each time he fights, he grows more formidable. Even Raknid might not be truly destroyed. He has eons in which to regenerate. But other vengeful dark entities will be hunting us now. . . ."

I said nothing; I had no words of comfort for Thorne, who truly needed them more than I did. Soon I would leave the dark, but she would have to stay behind, and the servants of the Fiend would continue to hunt her. Many were like Tanaki—they never gave up.

We got to our feet and set off again. Soon we were entering another cave. Then, after a series of tunnels and caverns, we emerged onto the white path again. This time there was no cave at its end, just a tiny green star that grew quickly to first become an orb and then, finally, an oasis of green floating in the abyss.

I had reached Pan's domain.

"Send my regards to my teacher, Grimalkin," Thorne said. "Tell her I am sorry that I faltered and betrayed you. But please let her know that I came back to help, that her words reached me in the dark, and that I have tried hard to become what she wished—as brave in death as I was in life!"

"You've tried and succeeded. Ain't no doubt about that,"

I said with a smile. "I'll tell her all that you did. How you took Beelzebub's thumb bones and stabbed Raknid in both eyes, then cut off his legs. She'll like that. Couldn't have done better herself!"

We stared at each other for a moment, and a lump came into my throat. Perhaps I didn't have long to live, but at least I would see earth once more. I was going home; Thorne was trapped in the dark forever—unless she eventually fell victim to one of its predators. And then she would be nothing. Her soul would be obliterated.

I headed toward that green oasis. Just before I entered it, I looked back. Thorne was walking away into the distance, getting smaller and smaller.

I felt really sad.

CHAPTER XXX
Good News and Bad

AS soon as I entered Pan's domain, I eased up my skirt and checked the mark on my thigh.

At first glance, I was terrified. It looked like the full dark moon that I had been warned about by Agnes Sowerbutts. But I felt no different, and on closer inspection it seemed to me that it was not *quite* grown to its maximum size.

There was still hope.

I walked on to find Pan, clothed in leaves and bark, sitting on a log playing a reed pipe, just as he had been the last time we talked. It was as if all the dangers I'd faced in the dark had been no more than a dream, and he had been waiting here for me to open my eyes and see him once more.

He was that same fair boy, pleasant to look upon, only his long pointy ears and green curly toenails marking him as other than human.

He smiled at me and lowered the pipes from his mouth. I smiled back.

"You were successful!" he cried, nodding toward the dagger at my belt.

"I hope so," I replied. "I have the blade I came for, but am I too late? How much time has passed back on earth? Halloween hasn't come and gone, has it?"

"It is the thirtieth of September. A month remains before Halloween. You are not too late. But before you return to your world, you must first pay the price of your presumption in entering my domain uninvited!"

"Then please tell me what it is," I said, holding my breath in fear of what he might demand.

He smiled again. "I have helped you. All I ask is that you help me."

"Help you . . . to do what?"

"For now it is not for you to know. In time I will tell you. The price is simple—just be ready to answer my call and give me the help I need. Whatever you are doing when you hear my pipes, come to me at once. Do you understand?"

"Yes, I understand," I replied, so desperate to find Tom that I would have agreed to anything.

"And will you do as I ask?"

"Yes. When I hear the pipes, I will come to you."

What else could I say? If I didn't agree, he would never let me go home.

"Then for now, return to the world and do what you must do!" he commanded.

Everything seemed to spin about me. I felt sick; I closed my eyes.

When I opened them again, I was sitting on the grass with my back against a tree. I was once more in the forest close to the river.

I was home.

I set off for Chipenden at once. I was looking forward to seeing Tom. We would have a little time together before the ritual—almost a month. I would have to make the best of it.

It was late afternoon, and the sun was warm overhead. It was good weather for the last day of September in the County. I could see the smoke from the village chimney pots rising above the trees. I took the path to the left, the one that would take me away from those houses and straight to the home of Old Gregory.

But on the slope, someone was waiting in the shadow of the trees.

It was Grimalkin.

How long had she been waiting here for me? No doubt she had scryed the likely time I'd emerge from the dark. I was relieved to see that she was still carrying the leather sack containing the Fiend's head. But she had something else in her left hand. It looked like a book—a slim one, bound in brown leather.

"I have good news for you, and bad," Grimalkin announced, straight out. She was grim faced, and my heart lurched.

"Is Tom all right?" I demanded, my voice wobbling with panic. "Nothing's happened to him, has it?"

"Tom is safe, Alice. What I have to tell you does not concern him at all. In fact, it's better that he doesn't know anything."

"What then? What's wrong?"

"The bad news is that you didn't need to journey into the dark after all. The dagger you hold is not needed. You risked your life and very soul for nothing. The good news is that you need not surrender your life to Tom's blades. You don't have to be sacrificed. I have found another way to destroy the Fiend."

I couldn't believe what I was hearing.

"Here," Grimalkin continued, holding out the book toward me. "This is all we need."

I felt a strange reluctance even to touch what she offered. As soon as it was within my hands, I knew why. In silver letters engraved into the brown cover was its title—a word that sent a chill into my heart.

DOOMDRYTE.

Also embossed in silver was an ominous image that I instantly recognized: the head and forelimbs of a skelt.

Those bloodthirsty creatures had played a big part in my life recently: the encounters with them in the dark; the skelt heads that formed the hilts of the hero swords; and now this cover. It seemed more than just a series of coincidences. What did they have to do with the destruction of the Fiend?

This book was the most powerful grimoire that had ever been written, and some believed it had been dictated to an ancient mage called Lukrasta by the Fiend himself. Every Pendle witch knew the potential of the Doomdryte, and a few had spent their lives searching for it. It contained just one very long spell that had to be recited without the slightest mistake, over a period of many hours. It was said that the successful reading of the spell, combined with certain rituals, would give the reader the powers of a god—invulnerability and immortality.

There was one problem. History demonstrated that to complete a perfect reading was impossible.

Everyone who had ever attempted the incantation had died in the process—including Lukrasta. Just one hesitation or mispronunciation, and that was the end of you.

"You have the strength and ability to do this, Alice," Grimalkin told me. "Use your magic to enhance your concentration and complete the incantation. Then, with what you draw from the Doomdryte, you will be able to destroy the Fiend."

I just stared at the witch assassin, not knowing how to reply. What she said was probably true. The power of the book and my own magical strength combined could well be enough to do what was necessary.

But at what cost to myself?

Would it be better to allow myself to be sacrificed after all?

But then Grimalkin told me something that made me put aside my own concerns.

"I also come to meet you with news of a great danger," she said. "I have been on a journey far to the north, where I encountered a strange nonhuman species called the Kobalos; they have powerful mages, able to wield strange magic that may eventually pose a threat to the County. They have the ability to create monstrous creatures, and they enslave human women because they have no females of their own."

"No females? How can that be possible?" I asked.

"They murdered all their own long ago," Grimalkin replied. "I fear that soon they will burst out of their northern territory and embark upon a war that will have dire consequences for humans. They will kill all our men and boys, and our women will become slaves. It is vital that we deal with the Fiend quickly and put an end to him once and for all. Once that is done, we can begin to prepare for that new threat. Alice, we must use the Doomdryte!"

⊙ ⊙ ⊙

It fills my heart with sadness to have approached so close to the house of Old Gregory without being able to greet Tom. I have missed him so much. . . . When Grimalkin guided me away from Chipenden, I thought my heart would burst with the pain of it.

But she is right. She has convinced me that we must use the Doomdryte. And this is something that we can tell neither Tom nor his master, because they would strive to prevent it.

I believe my magic will enable me to bring sufficient concentration to bear upon the recital of the long spell so that I may complete it successfully. That done, I will use the power I have acquired to destroy the Fiend.

But I know that the consequences for me will be terrible.

The mark on my skin will quickly become a dark full moon. I will be bound to the dark forever, a thing without conscience, compassion, or a shred of human feeling.

That is a more terrible sacrifice than to die at the hands of Tom Ward, but it is the course that I have embarked upon.

For now, the witch assassin and I are living in a ruined cottage not too far from the Spook's house. It is the place where I once stayed with Lizzie while she plotted the death of John Gregory, hoping to free Mother Malkin from the pit in his garden. It is from that cottage that I once set out and met Tom for the first time.

Now it is the place where I will triumph or die in the attempt.

I must be brave.

I must do what has to be done.

I am Alice.

FROM

THE LAST APPRENTICE

FURY OF THE SEVENTH SON

·BOOK THIRTEEN·

CHAPTER I
ANOTHER WAY

I awoke from a nightmare, my heart pounding, and sat up in bed feeling sick. For a few moments I thought I was going to vomit, but gradually my stomach settled down.

In my dream I had been killing Alice—cutting away her thumb bones.

At Halloween, now barely a month away, I would have to carry out this terrible ritual in the real world. It was what was expected of me. My mam wished it, for it was the only way to end the threat of the Fiend forever.

But how could I do it? How could I kill Alice?

I lay awake, fearful of going back to sleep lest the nightmare resume. Painful thoughts continued to swirl through my head. Alice was a willing victim. She was prepared to be sacrificed. Not only that, but she had bravely ventured into the dark to retrieve the Blade of Sorrow. This was one of the hero swords—three sacred weapons to be used to destroy the Fiend . . . weapons that would kill her in the process.

The hero swords had been forged by the Old God Hephaestus; the first of these was the Destiny Blade, given to me by Cuchulain in Ireland. The second was called Bone Cutter, and now, if Alice had succeeded in her quest into the dark, I would possess all three.

At the moment the Fiend was bound to his dead flesh—his body impaled with silver spears in the Irish countryside, his head in a leather sack in the possession of Grimalkin, the witch assassin. She was on the run, fighting desperately to keep it from the Fiend's servants. If they got hold of it, they would reunite head and body, and the Fiend would walk the earth once more, and the ritual could not take place.

But Alice had still not returned from the dark. Perhaps something had happened, I thought. Maybe she would never come back. . . .

I was also worried about my brother James, who had gone missing. The fiend had said that his servants had cut his throat and thrown him into a ditch. I desperately hoped he was lying, but I couldn't keep the terrible thought of it out of my head for long.

I tried to sleep again, without success, and the night dragged on. Then, just before dawn, the mirror on my bedside table suddenly began to glow. Alice was the only one who ever contacted me using a mirror. I sat up and grabbed it, looking into the glass, hardly daring to hope. For weeks and weeks I had been waiting for word from her. I had thought that perhaps I would see her just stroll happily into the garden, the Dolorous Blade in hand. But now Alice would be able to tell me that all was well immediately.

My heart soared with happiness as she stared out of the glass at me, a faint smile on her lips. She mouthed a sentence: "I'm on the edge of the western garden."

In the past I used to communicate with Alice by breathing on the glass and writing, but I had grown skilled at reading her lips. She had no difficulty at all in reading mine.

"Wait there!" I told her. "I'll be down right away."

I dressed quickly, then went downstairs as quietly as possible, trying not to wake the Spook. As I headed out through the back door, a thought struck me: Why hadn't Alice come into the garden?

The sky was growing lighter in the east, and as I passed the bench where my master sometimes gave me lessons, I saw Alice waiting at the edge of the trees.

She was dressed as I had last seen her—in a dark dress that just came down below her knees, and her pointy shoes. But what cheered me most of all was the smile on her pretty face. I ran toward her and she opened her arms, her smile broadening. We hugged each other tight and rocked back and forth.

"You're safe! You're safe!" I cried. "I never thought I'd see you again."

At last we broke apart and stared at each other silently for a moment or two.

"There were times when I thought I'd never escape from the dark," Alice said. "But I did it, Tom. I got in and out safely, and I have the blade. Glad to see you, I am."

She pulled it from a pocket and held it out to me. I turned it over and over in my hands, looking at it closely. It looked just like its twin, Bone Cutter: the same skelt with ruby eyes adorned the hilt, staring up at me. The skelt was a killer that hid in crevices near water before scuttling out on its eight legs to pierce its victims with its bone tube and drain their blood.

I forced my eyes away from the blade and looked again at Alice, feeling a surge of happiness. I'd missed her so much. How could I ever have considered sacrificing her? Even the destruction of the Fiend surely couldn't justify it. It was clear to me now that I couldn't go through with it. Tears came to my eyes and a lump to my throat.

"You're brave, Alice. Nobody else could have succeeded. But I'm sorry—you did it all for nothing. I can't go through with the ritual. I won't sacrifice you. I wouldn't hurt you for anything. We'll have to find another way to put an end to the Fiend."

"It's funny, Tom, but you're the second person to tell me that my going into the dark was unnecessary. Grimalkin thinks so, too."

"You've talked to Grimalkin? I haven't seen her in over a month."

"Grimalkin's been helping me. She's found another way to destroy the Fiend—we're working on it together. I'm hopeful, Tom. I really believe we can do it without the need for such a sacrifice. Had to come and see you and tell you, I did, but I've got to get back now. There's work to do."

I couldn't believe that Alice was already going off again.

We'd been apart for so long, and now all we'd had was a couple of minutes together. It was so disappointing. I wanted to know more about Grimalkin's plan. How had she discovered a method that Mam had not been aware of?

"Come back to the house for a while, please," I begged her. "Tell me what's going on. And I'd like to know how you coped in the dark—I'm sure the Spook will have all sorts of questions to ask you, too."

But Alice shook her head firmly. "That ain't possible, Tom. You see, Grimalkin's plan makes use of seriously dark magic. It's the only thing that'll work. Old Gregory wouldn't approve, you know that. He's bound to ask me questions about what I'm up to, and I'd have to lie to him. He's good at telling when people are lying. It's best that I go."

"Then when will I see you again, Alice?"

"Ain't sure, but Grimalkin and I will return for sure. . . . See you when we've succeeded."

Alice looked just as I remembered her, but as she spoke now, she sounded different—completely confident of success. Was she being overconfident?

"Is it dangerous?" I asked nervously.

"I won't lie to you, Tom. Of course it's dangerous. But we've been in danger from the dark from the moment we met, and we've always come through safely. Don't see why this shouldn't be the same."

Suddenly she rushed into my arms and kissed me fiercely on the lips. Before I could respond, it was over; she broke away from me and began to walk off.

I stared after her in shock. I was stunned. Why had she kissed me? Could it really be that she cared for me as much as I cared for her? I had never known. I desperately wanted to hold her in my arms again.

Alice turned, looked back, and called out over her shoulder, "Take care, Tom! Don't tell Old Gregory you've seen me. It's best that way."

And then she was gone. There was so much I hadn't had time to ask her. What had it been like in the dark? How had she managed to survive and retrieve the blade I now held in my hand?

I walked back toward the house sadly. I was very relieved that Alice had returned safely, but now I had something else to worry about. What were Alice and Grimalkin about to attempt? No doubt there were great risks involved.

She'd asked me not to tell my master that I'd met her. One part of me agreed with her; it was probably for the best to keep it from him—he'd only ask questions. But I'd kept too many things from him in the past. I'd have to hide the blade to make sure he didn't see it.

I'd been feeling increasingly guilty about such deceptions. Each had seemed very necessary at the time, but they had accumulated, and the more there were, the worse I'd felt. This was one more to add to the list, and I didn't like it.

CHAPTER II
THE SPOOK'S LEGACY